THE BIRTHDAY BUYER

THE BIRTHDAY BUYER

ADOLFO GARCÍA ORTEGA

Translated from the Spanish by
Peter Bush

 Hispabooks
Publishing

Hispabooks Publishing, S. L.
Madrid, Spain
www.hispabooks.com

Originally published in Spain as *El comprador de aniversarios* by
Seix Barral, 2008
First published in English by Hispabooks, 2013
English translation copyright © by Peter Bush
Design and Photography © Simonpates - www.patesy.com

A CIP record for this book is available from the British Library

ISBN 978-84-941744-5-2 (trade paperback)
ISBN 978-84-941744-6-9 (ebook)
Legal Deposit: M-32003-2013

Schwarze Milch der Frühe wir trinken dich nacht wir trinken dich
mittags der Tod ist ein Meister aus Deutschland.

[Black milk of dawn we drink you at night we drink you at noon
Death is a Master in Germany.]

PAUL CELAN

CONTENTS

I

THE TOOTH PULLERS

1

Auschwitz is too close.

If Hurbinek, for example, had survived, he would be fifty-nine. He really wouldn't be that old, and he might have a good memory, a cruelly good memory that would prompt those horrific nightmares so often experienced by people who passed through the camps when they are devoured by hunger, by hunger and yet more hunger. His grandchildren would still be youngsters, at most adolescents who respected him highly. He'd have a good job, suited to his physical condition, in Poland or Hungary or perhaps a Russian city, and it would be early days to hear talk of retirement. No, Auschwitz is still too close. It isn't as unreal as Trafalgar, the French Revolution or Waterloo often seem in textbooks. There are survivors. Although Hurbinek isn't one of them.

Hurbinek. Who would Hurbinek be today if he had survived?

Well, of course, I could be incredibly abstract and miss out Auschwitz, its Nazi horrors, the crematoria, the gas chambers, the cattle trucks arriving on snow-swept nights, the screams and merciless harshness, the planning that went into those factories for the mass production of Jewish corpses and cripples. Much has already been written about that. I'm not even sure I will let myself be tempted by the symbolic status the huge extermination camp of Auschwitz Birkenau now bears as a pivotal point in history, or by what Adorno said—which wasn't true—that it was impossible to write poetry after Auschwitz: subsequently many more people have been—and are still being—exterminated and lots of poetry is still being written.

I can choose to be abstract and only speak about Hurbinek.

I only want to speak about him.

Only about him.

Today no one more than he deserves words, and language. And that is because Hurbinek is the most horrendous symbol of silence that History could ever have created.

I want Hurbinek to exist.

To exist once more. To exist for longer. To be an existence that endures.

To lead an invented, possible life. Manufactured by me.

What use is an invented life to him?

Perhaps it is of no use at all to him if someone were to invent his life. Dead at the age of three, he never learned what life was about, though he clung desperately on to the last scrap of minuscule energy his minuscule, paralyzed body could create. But it is of use to me, in no small way, to invent his life. It is the only path to redemption both he and I can take. I am, as it were, giving life to Hurbinek. Yes, that is what I'm doing, come to think of it.

2

I was going to Auschwitz, but not anymore.

I have only faint memories of the following: at 4 p.m. one Saturday afternoon I paid for a full tank at counter 7 in a Shell service station on the A-3 Motorway, then jumped back in my Ford, switched on a Leonard Cohen cassette ("Lover, lover, lover"), read a sign in front that said "Frankfurt-Main/Autobahn A-5" and decided I should leave the A-3 Motorway for the A-5 (the turnoff was very clear, just three hundred feet away), when a truck transporting tires suddenly banged into the back of my car and shot me off the road. I turned over several times and lost consciousness.

They said my car was a write-off. The insurance would see to everything. The truck driver didn't pass the alcohol test. He was speeding. They said he only dislocated a foot.

I was going to Auschwitz, but not anymore.

On the contrary, I'm in a Frankfurt hospital, the Universitäts-Kliniken, on the Theodor Sternstrasse, opposite the river. I was travelling alone on this trip. Fanny stayed at home with the girls. It was going to be a long, uncomfortable, hardly fun journey. "It may be a pilgrimage, but it's not tourism. How can one turn Auschwitz into a tourist thing?" I'd say defensively. I couldn't tell you why, but *I had* to go alone, to feel *alone* there. I now know I won't make it to Auschwitz, that the final half of my journey has to be postponed to another time, I hope.

The medical report they read me says I have two broken legs, two fractured ribs, severe bruising, a swollen right cheek and occasionally vomit blood they are checking to make sure there isn't something internal that's not working properly. When I'm recovered, I'll take a plane home. I was going to Auschwitz, but not anymore.

3

I didn't lead Fanny to panic. I don't want to worry her or the girls. She's capable of rushing here with the pair of them. After all, these doctors have everything under control. It won't be long, a couple of weeks at most. I'm sharing a small ward with five other people. It's not very welcoming. It's more like a place of transit, a ward that's been improvised from a mismatch of old furniture. The windows are high up and barred. You can see a strip of sky, and if I sit up in bed I can catch a glimpse of the odd roof and church steeple. My five roommates are all German but seem middle or working-class. It's no private hospital. That's clear from the meals they bring up and the sparse selection of objects in the ward, some of which are broken or shabby.

I've always dreaded hospitals. They make me feel sick. I know this phobia has a name, that it is a clinical phobia and affects lots of people. It's panic sparked off by that sweeping sterility where one feels one is lost and drifting, in an echoing void, a place of childish imaginary torture, where metallic sounds unexpectedly reverberate, with that color white that permeates everything, walls, uniforms, bandages, a white where the red blood can suddenly appear even more violently because it is expected, cold, deliberate.

Only Primo Levi has spoken about Hurbinek. He was in a hospital ward, as I am now, except for the drastic difference that his hospital (a name it hardly deserves) was located in a corner of the Main Camp in Auschwitz. "All the same, my attention," writes Primo Levi in *The Truce*, "and that of my neighbors in the nearby beds, rarely managed to escape from the obsessive presence and mortal power of affirmation, of the smallest and most harmless among us: of a child, of Hurbinek." And a couple of pages later he will add: "Nothing remains of him: he bears witness through these words of mine."

Silence. Emptiness. And gratitude: mine, and that of thousands like me. If it weren't for the words that Primo Levi devotes to Hurbinek, the passage through life of that small three-year-old boy, crippled from the waist downward, would have been swallowed up by oblivion. Like so many millions of others. But Hurbinek struggled against oblivion, as his body struggled against death until his strength failed him.

I feel strangely alone in this hospital ward. These young German doctors make me feel anxious when they approach my bed every now and then, listen to my heartbeat, smile for a second and mouth syllables similar to those millions of men, women and children heard in the camps, as they were being exterminated. Of course, I know they are not saying the same things. Or are they? Because the children sent to the hospital so they could experiment every manner of crazy, sadistic madness on their frail, shaking bodies for the greater good of German science under Dr. Mengele would have been spoken to in similar terms to the ones they now use with me: "Lift your arm up," "Bring your arm down," "Open your mouth," "Does that hurt?" "Turn over," "This is swollen," "Bandage," "Cut," "Open," "Extract."

They are the same words used by the tooth pullers who extracted teeth from Jews before they were sent to the gas chambers. With great precision, using their strength, breaking only the mouths of Jews. Besides, the pain would make them forget their fear. Or at least that's what the tooth pullers thought. I know, the difference is the context in which they are said. Except that in some remote corner of my subconscious contexts become blurred: a state hospital in Frankfurt and an infirmary in Auschwitz, or in Dachau, or in Buchenwald, or in Treblinka, or in Majdanek, or in Sobibor, or in Chelmno. Perhaps what the contexts share in my subconscious, terrifyingly, are the short, guttural, sibilant German words. Uttered unemotionally, clinically, technically, the sounds are identical in my Frankfurt hospital and any of the experimental laboratories run by those Nazi doctors.

The very same words Hurbinek heard at some time in that short life of his without understanding anything at all.

4

I have been wanting to write about Hurbinek for years, though I didn't realize it was Hurbinek I wanted to write about. I don't know how old I was when I saw the first photographs, the first images on film of Nazi extermination camps but I must have been a kid. It was shocking. Now I can't remember if I saw photos my father showed me in a book on the Second World War or if it was a television documentary about the Allies reaching the camps: ghostly, wandering bodies, human skin and bone, wrapped in blankets, looking out lifelessly from the deadly skulls their faces had become. Those pictures made such a deep impression that later on, over the years, I decided I wanted to probe the reasons behind that massacre, that annihilation, to find out who the guilty parties were and who the victims were, to ascertain the historical truth. I wanted to know the *details*. I read eyewitness accounts, I sought out eyewitnesses, I visited some of the scenes. I felt I was Jewish, Russian or any of the victims of persecution, humiliation and elimination, human beings crushed and erased simply because they existed. Murdered because they existed. I felt like a victim, any one of those victims. And of those victims, Hurbinek perhaps was most victim of all.

The heaps were always what most shocked me in what I saw and read at the time. Huge heaps of shoes, buckles, hats, watches, coats, suitcases, beards, teeth and molars. I was horrified to see those piles of thousands upon thousands of molars and teeth, and men separating the ones with gold fillings from the rest. Their handy work, their smiling, conscientious faces and keen focus on what they were doing made them seem to me like monsters: their actions were so everyday, so normal. Then Hannah Arendt coined the exact term to define such an attitude: the banality of evil. When I later decided to write about Hurbinek, I knew I was legitimized by a sense of justice, but I couldn't find

15

the words. There are words one cannot find simply because they do not and cannot exist.

5

What do we know about Hurbinek? Nothing. We only have the scant information Primo Levi gives us in the second book that he devotes to recording his experience in the Nazi camps.

The war was in its final phase: on January 27, 1945 the first Russian patrol reaches the Buna-Monowitz Lager within the orbit of Auschwitz Birkenau; Primo Levi and other sick people are moved to the Main Camp in Auschwitz; there the Russians have set up a "ward for the infectious," a ward two or three times bigger than the one where I am now in Frankfurt, that crammed in eight hundred sick people; Primo Levi is feverish and delirious and is moved to a smaller place; there, on one of the bunks, is a three-year-old child they have named Hurbinek, interpreting thus some of the strange sounds he sporadically blurts out; his legs are atrophied and his eyes are his only grasp on life: "they struck the living like darts," says Levi. "It was a stare both savage and human."

Perhaps he was Russian or Hungarian; lots of Hungarians came to the camps in those last months, when the Red Army was only a few miles away and they had accelerated the process of gassing and cremating in the ovens.

Perhaps he was Polish and his mother gave birth to him right there in the camp.

Perhaps Auschwitz was his only universe in those long three years.

The atrophy in his legs must have been caused by cold and neglect: no doubt someone tried to eliminate him when he was born and didn't succeed. His own mother? Quite possibly. Driven by pity she tried to choke him with the threadbare clothes she wore. She couldn't. Hurbinek resisted. Perhaps she gave him to someone else, who in a rush grabbed his legs like a runt, dislocated them from his hips and dropped him through a hole in the floorboard, out of the barracks into the bad weather. He survived the snow because nobody could silence him. Under the barracks or next to the latrines or wherever it was they chose to leave him to die, nobody managed to stay put long enough to cover his mouth and asphyxiate him. Someone soon picked him up, on the sly. He screamed too much. And he didn't go back to his mother. He never went back to his mother. Perhaps his mother had already killed herself, or died during his birth, or died on the vast esplanade, during the roll call, exhausted by the blood she lost giving birth, or died as a result of the whim of the *Kapo* who whipped her guts out. The range of possibilities ever broadens . . . From barracks to barracks, from one woman to another, from one man to another, who can say, undernourished and sick, surviving from birth on a mixture of strength and chance that would endure three agonizing years. News of his existence soon reached the ears of the SS: perhaps someone told the barrack's *Kapo* about the newborn child, another of the many who had survived the abortion or strangulation attempted by his mother or father, the low temperatures, the game the SS liked to play shooting at

17

them spiked on a post of the barbed wire fence as if they were a cloth rabbit at a fairground. No one knows or will ever know when they tattooed a number on his arm.

Perhaps he was Jewish.

6

I repeat: what do we know about Hurbinek? Nothing really. An eloquent, horrible nothing, but it is a nothing in general. What do we know about one another? Nothing. Or everything, because life itself reproduces us and we reproduce life, and in turn we reproduce each other in life, we replicate and imitate each other. We are united by what is most private and separated by what is superficial. We all perform the same way: we won't know the specific facts (where you were born, where you live, how much you earn, who your parents, grandparents etc. are, what your street, your telephone number, your profession etc. is), but we do know how you will react to pain, anguish, loneliness and fear. And if we don't know how people react in extreme conditions, how millions perished at the hands of the Nazis, at least we know enough to understand the pain, anguish, loneliness and fear felt by others. We feel compassion; we are human. But are we? Now isn't Eichmann also perhaps human, the organiser of the extermination, a manufacturer of corpses for bureaucratic purposes, because that is what he is ordered to do and that is what he does as a good German paterfamilias, because it is his role in the machinery of the Third Reich? And isn't Adolf Hitler perhaps human when he weeps, distraught, when his mother Klara dies, and isn't that what his doctor, Eduard Bloch, his surgeon, who in forty years in medicine had never seen a man so deeply and painfully affected "in such circumstances" thinks? After forty years in his profession, with thousands of patients dying in his care, was the sorrow of young Adolf Hitler the only sorrow ever to make an impression on Dr. Bloch? And what do I know about Hitler? Nothing. What did Hurbinek know about Hitler? Nothing. What did the millions of human beings Hitler condemned to die know about him? Nothing. What did the people living in Germany know about the dead? Nothing. Or almost nothing. I take another look around: I am in hospital in Frankfurt; they are taking care of me, I don't want to be unfair. But I am afraid that the grandfather or uncle or great-grandfather of that young, fair-featured doctor who looks at me coldly every day did know mass murder was carried out by Germans, by their children, by their brothers, by their husbands; they knew, in any case, at least, that an anonymous Polish child would be born in a camp that had been expressly built in order to eliminate him, to eradicate him from this world. It wouldn't be difficult to imagine, if they had given it just a little bit of thought. Even if they didn't know he would be called Hurbinek. And that the memory of him would last more than any memory of the vast majority of themselves.

7

I have devotingly read the books written by Primo Levi and have been captivated, horrified and filled with admiration.

I have read his stories, his wonderful tales. I was struck with awe when I read his autobiographical writing about his long journey to the hell of Auschwitz that begins in 1943 when the fascists arrested him in the Aosta Valley. First *If This Is a Man*, then *The Truce*, and finally *The Drowned and the Saved*. Shortly after writing this last book, in April 1987, he threw himself down the stairwell from the third floor of his house. He died from the injuries sustained in that brutal fall. He was sixty-eight years old.

There is a photo of him in the glove compartment of my shattered Ford that is now in one of the car pounds run by the Frankfurt *polizei*. It is dedicated to me. He had been awarded the Campiello Prize for a second time for *If Not Now, When?* It was December 1982 and work had taken me to Turin. I remember it was dusk and that I went for a long stroll. There was a throng milling around beside a shop window in a small square. I went over and to my surprise I saw Primo Levi inside signing copies of his most recent book. I didn't have a copy but he very kindly took a photo of himself from a leather wallet and wrote his name and mine and the date on it. I had no choice but to take that photo with me on my journey to re-tell—as if in a modest, personal homage—the life of a three-year-old boy who only ever experienced suffering. The photo of the guardian of his memory.

The taciturn, peaceful look on his face augurs his suicide. He deceived no one. Like Jean Améry. Like Paul Celan. Like many other anonymous survivors who decided to stop re-inventing themselves day by day.

Hurbinek was dumb. Or couldn't speak. He'd make a supreme effort writhing his small triangular face as his eye sockets sunk down deeper and deeper, and he made only sounds, scraps of syllables, words that nobody understood. They might be moans, might be snatches of a song he had heard, might be the word that held his real name, always a mere approximation, always voiced by a terrified child who wants to live at any cost. If in fact what Hurbinek wanted, what floated in his eyes *was* the intense desire to speak, to explode in sounds, alongside his unspeakable exhaustion, total absence of energy, when it seemed every breath would be his last, the last drop of life fleeing as he gasped and panted, when his tiny lungs went anxiously up and down, always at the point of collapse.

A six-figure number had been clumsily tattooed on his arm.

He was paralytic, couldn't swivel his hips and his legs were two sticks without any muscle that barely if ever managed to support him.

9

I have always been left astounded by the kind, peaceful looks on the faces of aged Nazi murderers in their old age or when they appear in public accused of a crime against humanity. Hunted for years, then discovered, arrested and held while awaiting trial, those murderers are transformed in the process. They become faces worthy of compassion and benevolence. Like those belonging to the Eichmanns or Barbies or Pinochets or Pol-Pots when they are being tried (or in the future to Karadzic, Mladic and Milosevic, or the Ruandans Kabunga, Renzaho and Bizimungu). They seem good, innocent people, alien to everything they are accused of. It is then that I remember the mountains and mountains of teeth and molars I saw in that documentary when I was a child. It is then that the tooth pullers come to the foreground of my mind.

And then I think of a similar face, our family dentist's, when I was a child. That tooth puller must have been a real Nazi, I recall, because he would tell me or one of my brothers: "Don't complain, at least I give you an anesthetic. Think about the Jews when their molars were simply wrenched out." At the time neither my brothers nor I understood what that enigmatic story told by our affable, gray-haired dentist referred to, the resigned warning of someone who knows more than he is letting on. Now, of course, we all know what he meant.

II

THE TEAR AT THE END OF MY NAIL

1

I make an effort. My legs hurt; the powerful painkiller given me by the elderly nurse made its impact some time ago; the plaster casts are enormously irritating. But what is my *small-scale* grief compared to the *infinite* suffering of Primo Levi or Hurbinek? I wonder in my hospital bed. I make an effort to push myself up on my elbows and sit on the bed; I stretch my neck; in the distance, through the barred window I can see the winged crests of the sculptures of the Alte Oper. It has all been rebuilt—so I've been told—the whole city is new, remade after the war. Bombing raids destroyed Frankfurt. In 1944 the wife and children of Heinz Rügen, the *SS Obergruppenführer* who applied for a post in Auschwitz Birkenau, lived on a broad or narrow street—I'm not sure which—near the Alte Oper.

Against his best wishes Heinz Rügen wasn't able to celebrate Christmas with his family on December 24, 1944, the day he wrote a letter, his last, to his wife and children; the letter has been preserved and is highly affectionate, moving even. It ends with a beautiful image: "As I write to you, a tear has dropped onto my finger and is rolling down to the end of my nail. It slips onto the paper. I'm sending it to you even though it will be dry by the time it reaches you." He signed and folded it and put it in an envelope emblazoned with a swastika that he popped into the pocket of his uniform. The Russian soldier who shot him a month later found it there, in the truck that Rügen was riding in, abandoning the death camp where he had so desired to serve the Führer. But before that, that same day when he wrote the letter, on Christmas Eve, Heinz Rüger, well bundled up, left the guard post. It was very cold. He lifted his hand to touch the pocket with the letter, perhaps reminding himself he shouldn't forget to leave it in the office out-tray or tenderly remembering his beloved ones at home. He approached barrack 346. He strode toward one of the bunks. He pushed out a woman who was probably young but looked aged. Nobody knows who she was, but she was Ángela Pérez León, a Spanish Sephardic Jew married to a train driver from Bohemia whom she'd not seen ever since she'd come to the camp. The woman was clutching a little body that didn't cry at all when she fell. Rügen dragged her out of the barrack and shot her in the nape of her neck near the door. The bullet came out through her nose. Then he grabbed the baby by an arm and hurled it into the distance as if it were a doll. Hurbinek flew through the air. Rügen thought he wouldn't waste another bullet, the heavy snow that was falling would be enough to finish off the little monster. To an extent he was carrying out the order he had given that very morning that his men had apparently ignored. He was tired of seeing that kid's paralytic body time and again. How could it still be alive? Heinz Rügen couldn't think about his children and be forced to see that scum, day in day out. Now the Russians were at the gates to the camp he ought to quickly complete the task he had undertaken. The tear at the end of my nail, he thought.

The three-year-old kid shivered on the snow, on the central roadway, until Henek picked him up later.

2

Rügen died in the truck taking him and his men to the old German border after they had abandoned to their fate the walking corpses that remained in the camp. He was one of the last to leave. Others had already departed, and taken the healthy prisoners with them on forced marches that left a trail of dead on the roads. The bullet hit him in the chest and the impact made him fall off the truck. His troops abandoned him there; nobody could do anything for him and the driver preferred to speed on his way.

The chaos of Auschwitz didn't disappear when the Russians arrived. There is confusion, a constant noise of shouting and praying, some happy, some indignant, others hardly able to overcome their state of paralysis and denied humanity. They no longer know that they are men because they have long ceased to be. Those who can walk, go to and fro through mud and snow. Nobody speaks to them. Nobody worries about anyone. The Soviet soldiers simply look on, awkwardly, as if they were at the gates to hell.

They don't dare act as liberators. They don't understand what their eyes can see. Nobody gives orders. The inmates don't understand what is happening, although they all—most of them dying—know that the SS have gone and that that is a good thing.

They improvised an infirmary at one corner of the esplanade, in a shack previously used by the guards for executions by hanging. The less seriously sick had to look after the others. There were no doctors, only Soviet or Polish nurses to-ing and fro-ing, unable to do anything, terrified and disgusted by what they found with every step they took. They set up a line of twenty bunks in the shack with very thin straw mattresses.

Buczko, the cobbler, a thirty-four-year-old native of Pomerania stricken with dysentery, carried the prisoner Primo Levi in his arms: Levi had a raging temperature, was delirious and couldn't walk by himself. He was from the Buna-Monowitz camp.

The schoolteacher from Radzyn, Rubem Yetzev, fifty-five, with horrific rheumatism in all his joints, was looking after three sick inmates who had dragged themselves that far. Rubem Yetzev had carried them one by one over his shoulders along the last stretch to the infirmary, put them on bunks and then stretched out on one himself. The three men were Abrahan Levine, Elias Achtzehn and Ernst Sterman, and were suffering respectively from diphtheria, acute typhoid and tuberculosis. The first two were to die in the shack.

The ice-cream manufacturer, Chaim Roth, forty-seven, born in Katowice, looked after Ira his brother, who had gone out of his mind and kept biting his hands.

Henek, fifteen, a worker from Transylvania in Hungary, carried the three-year-old he'd rescued from the snow on Christmas Eve, wrapped up in an SS overcoat. He had been looking after him ever since. The child struggled to breathe and only his restless eyes had any life. His eyes weren't sad, but anguished, weren't blank but insistent. He said nothing, except for a strange word that Henek interpreted as Hurbinek.

The rest of the sick were: Prosper Andlauer (French), Franz Patzold (Bohemian), Jan Vesely (Hungarian), Ahmed Yildirim (Slovakian), Manuel Valiño (Spanish), David Bogdanowski (Polish), Joseph Grosselin (French), Auguste Friedel (French), Konrad Egger (German) and Berek Goldstein (Polish).

3

The bunk is made from a plank of old, unplaned pinewood. The sparse mattress smells of damp and rot, the same sweet smell that permeates the whole camp, the smell of decomposing bodies. Covered in a blanket made from remnants of filthy, striped jackets, Hurbinek lies there quiet, defenceless, almost still, looking nervously toward the ceiling and sometimes all about him, his mouth open and round and like a fish's. He never stops shaking, he never has, he's been shaking his entire little life. By his side Henek strokes his forehead, talks to him and smiles. He has stayed with him ever since he furtively retrieved him from the central roadway, and with a nimbleness Henek still retains though nobody knows how he manages it. He

27

warmed him with his own body heat and held him to his chest as long as he could, even hid him until the SS ran off, still whimsically killing as they drove along in their cars.

Hiding that body wasn't difficult.

Hurbinek clutches one of his fingers. Henek tries to play a kind of game and tries to prop Hurbinek up, but he can't support himself. His little body hardly takes up a third of the bunk under his blanket. His badly shaven head spotted with sores is visible, and under the blanket his lungs can be made out, going up and down, but then there's nothing, as if there was no more body beyond that small thorax. His skinny legs seem crushed, non-existent, artificial.

Hiding such a body isn't difficult.

4

"Hurbinek was a nobody," writes Primo Levi, "a child of death, a child of Auschwitz."

When they asked Henek about that child, he invented a new story every time. He's my brother, he'd say, or he is the son of a Russian woman I met a year ago, he'd say, or the son of a man who just died and who left him to me, he'd say, another Hungarian like me.

Hurbinek's voice was almost inaudible. Its sounds were all mixed up with his asthmatic gasps as he panted and tried to breathe. Henek discerned the word Hurbinek in that timid, faint death rattle, repeated time and again, as if it were all he could say. Those syllables took shape on his parched lips, hur-bi-neck. That's his name, Henek said, an affirmation to inject greater realism into the stories he was inventing about the origins of that kid who clung on to life and defeated death. He's with me, Henek always added, as if he were still afraid someone might try to snatch him away. Henek wanted to look after Hurbinek. He had become his reason to live.

I'm trying to be punctilious over the detail, I would hate to leave anything out now I have decided to give life to my small child. From my bed in Frankfurt I now see Hurbinek's pale, terrified face, that ashen or gray earthy color people acquired in Auschwitz. I can see him now, I really can. I only have to close my eyes and touch my body underneath these sheets, in this hospital, to imagine the shape of Hurbinek's body. My knee is enough. What would Hurbinek's knee have been like? It is starting to obsess me. What *were* Hurbinek's knees like? A tear at the end of my nail.

5

I think Hurbinek lived just that length of time not to have memories, the time about which nobody could say I did such and such, went to such a place, felt such an emotion. Except for rare exceptions, all our memories begin *after* we are three, not before. That's why I'm horrified to think that Hurbinek, with all his strength and desire to live, only experienced a pre-life, only lived a strange extension of his mother's uterus. And yet all he lived in that time without memories was the permanent suffering, pain and fear that were his food, his playthings, the air he breathed.

Henek soon gave up on the daily exercises to restore life to Hurbinek's atrophied legs. It wasn't about whether blood was circulating through them or not, or whether they'd frozen or not, and that was why it made no sense rubbing them as much as Henek did. He only managed to warm them slightly. His legs never grew, it was as simple as that. Perhaps as a result of some congenital failing or kind of torture, his legs were always spindly like that. His legs grew at a different pace, if what happened to Hurbinek can be graced by the word "growth." Skinny, very skinny, limply hanging from his hips, without bones to join them to his hips, as if skin alone had joined them to his torso and they had then become dislocated and cut off from the rest of his body. Hurbinek's legs were like a ragdoll's. Henek was familiar with the circuses in Budapest during the city's great summer fairs, and was reminded of those puppets hanging on strings manipulated by a puppeteer in a Punch and Judy show. Hurbinek's legs were always very cold and his tiny, tiny feet were frozen and pretty.

He'd raise his arms very slowly and his gaunt face twitched with pain when his arms were high enough to hug Henek's neck. It took a long time for that to happen. When Hurbinek hugged or seemingly hugged Henek and the latter felt on his cheek a light kiss or something similar, Henek, who was now experiencing similar symptoms of dysentery to Primo Levi and the other inmates there, went out into the yard and dragged his feet as he ran, as if he were engaged in a half-hearted march rather than a proper race. He would weep, in an Auschwitz where nobody wept anymore. A tear at the end of his nail.

6

Hurbinek's eyes are dark and large.

Or seem to be large because his face has shrunk. One could say the flesh is slowly departing from Hubinek's face.

On the other hand, his eyes are still growing.

Hurbinek's eyes never stop moving. They look out or yearn. All his reactions to stimulation are painful, everything his senses feel hurts. Whatever he hears, whatever they put on his tongue, whatever he touches or smells. Everything perplexes him, remains unexplained, and above all he has to respond using his scant energy to struggle to the edge of the next minute of his life. He needs to know but doesn't know what he should know. His eyes say it all, laden with questions. Primo Levi often goes over to him. They both look at each other but they don't see the same thing. The Italian strokes the child's face. He helps Henek when it is time to look after him, and cleans away the dribble that forms at the corner of his lips. He gives him water but Hurbinek does not eat or drink. He throws everything up.

Hurbinek's face is angular, is sunken, has hollow depressions everywhere, and seems transparent. Primo Levi writes how the eyes in that face want "to break out of the tomb of his dumbness."

Hurbinek's eyes are a language in themselves.

7

I try to remember what my daughters were like when they were three years old. They simply never tired of playing; their words began to be tinged with irony, they spoke in sentences using the wrong words, chattered, were amusing and happy. They wanted everything and asked for everything. They needed words. They needed to talk and talk and talk. They were affectionate, ran to me, and kissed me as they clambered onto my shoulders. They were whimsical, could be annoying, called out unsuitedly in the middle of the night. They were loving, liked to blackmail, amuse, seduce, were nice to smell and their skin was firm and smooth. Carrying them to bed in my arms made me feel tremendously tender. I read them stories and watched them sleep peacefully, in their secure, rounded world. They had frights and I eased them away. I was at their side. They weren't alone. And they always knew that.

Could Hurbinek . . . ?

"His stare clamored with explosive urgency," writes Primo Levi. "It was a stare both savage and human, even mature, a judgement, which none of us could support, so heavy was it with force and anguish."

8

I love Henek. His life is terrible, I know, but I love him. He was barely a young man, just fifteen years old, and had already killed lots of men, all Romanians, with his father, according to Primo Levi, on the border with Romania where he lived and worked in a factory. His whole family had died in Auschwitz. He'd been in the children's barracks. They didn't last long there, they soon ended up in the hands of the doctors who experimented on them, or sent them straight to the gas chambers. What use were children in Auschwitz? Henek managed to become the *Kapo* in that barrack and saved many children from being sent to either of those two fateful ends. Even so, he paid a high price: whenever an SS came and gave him the order, he had to select the ones who were to die. It was a way to survive, he told Primo Levi, without any scruples.

Henek's dysentery attack wasn't as serious as that of others in the infirmary-shack. He was short but sturdy, and helped everyone a little, but spent most of the day next to Hurbinek. I find what binds me to Henek is his love for Hurbinek. That's why I love him, because he plays my role in relation to Hurbinek and is my vicarious past before History: he represents me. Or at least that is my guilty wish as someone who doesn't want to forget. I love Henek because I want to be Henek. I don't know what portion of Humanity Henek is, but I do know that without him, without Henek, what Adorno said would be absolutely right, that after Auschwitz it would have been impossible to write poetry. Or anything else.

He is there. He has made a cradle for Hurbinek, something more suited to his body, that keeps him warmer. On that huge, dirty bunk the child was always trembling. Now his trembling blurs with his spasmodic breathing, but at least he doesn't seem to be cold. But there's no doing away with the cold and hunger. Hunger in particular. They organized to try to get a supply of food. The Russians provide better soup than was on offer from the SS, but it's not enough, and besides their bodies aren't ready to eat very much. Hurbinek can hardly keep any food down.

They don't know what's wrong with him, perhaps he is completely atrophied and his digestive system doesn't work. Perhaps the rest of his body, except for his eyes, has decided to die. And that *is* what is happening. Henek keeps touching him, cuddling him, talking to him, telling him things, kissing his little arms, cleaning his clothing, removing his black excrement, and covering the sores that are all over his body.

I love Henek because he loves Hurbinek.

He reminds him of his Dora, his four-year-old sister, who was also sick and vulnerable, who didn't last more than half an hour in Auschwitz. At 3:00 a.m., the minute they arrived, all the children in the truck were led by the hand to the gas chamber. They walked in fear and laughed in fear, and Henek watched. Their faces had the same fear that now comes to Hurbinek's face whenever Henek disappears from sight.

I love Henek because a day didn't go by when he didn't try to make Hurbinek laugh, in the hope that he might just once. But he always failed.

9

One night Henek cut himself on a rusty piece of tin. It was a long gash that ran the whole length of his thumb to the palm of his hand. He was afraid it would get infected so he went to see one of the Polish nurses that occasionally visited the shack. They could only supply him with caustic soda. He applied it to his cut, and burnt himself so badly that he put his right hand out of action.

He sometimes saw rats when he left the shack to get a drop of soup for Hurbinek. The rats were tasty, according to the Polish nurses, but he had never tried rat meat. He discovered it was a dish that was much sought after by the Russians and by those they had recently liberated from Auschwitz. He managed to kill two rats with one blow from a stick. He used his own useless hand as bait to catch them. The rats sidled over to sniff the wound and Henek dropped a sack over them and beat them to death. He took them to Hurbinek so he could see the two dead rats. A Russian photographed Hurbinek with one of the dead rats at the foot of his cradle. They gave Henek a bigger ration of soup and tinned meat.

Buczko the cobbler brings him two bottles of water a day.

Yetzev the schoolmaster changes the patients' dressings whenever he bumps into the Polish nurses and they give him a supply of bandages.

Roth the ice-cream manufacturer helps Primo Levi to take those who have died in their bunks on to the path outside.

Henek teaches Hurbinek words for things he has never known and will never know. His aim is to get him to speak Hungarian. He says, "This is a tree," "This is a house," "This is a cat." "This is a mother," "This is a sun." He says, "This is a hat," "This is a river," "There are bridges over rivers," "This is a cake." He says, "Hurbinek loves Henek, Henek loves Hurbinek." He says, "This is an elephant," and every day, with infinite patience, ignoring his useless hand, Henek makes a grotesque imitation of an elephant, and makes a mud cake, and draws a river and bridge on the earthen floor of the shack, and turns a tin into a hat, and points to the sun when the sun comes out, and imitates a cat meowing, and builds a cardboard house for him. But he can never explain to him what a tree is or what a mother is.

Henek believes in the power of words, but not one could penetrate the eyes of Hurbinek, who understood nothing, shivered, and only wanted that being speaking those sounds so slowly to stay with him for ever and never let go of his hand. And Henek never stopped talking so Hurbinek would learn.

10

Hanka Silewski and Jadzia Tryzna are two Polish nurses who are not yet twenty. When they call in at the infirmary-shack, they visit Hurbinek's cradle and caress his fingers and face; they say he reminds them of the dolls they had in their childhood in Warsaw, something they think is so distant though it was only a few years ago. Even so, appalled by everything they have seen, there is love in the kisses they shower him with and in the clean clothes they bring just for him. But they can't think what else to do when by his side. They overwhelm him and when he looks at them, they don't want their eyes to meet the gaze of that child struggling to lift his neck up and mutter unintelligible sounds. Hurbinek's gaze unsettles them. They'd rather not love him. Besides, Jadzia can't get the image out of her head of what she found in one of the wards when she entered the camp with the Red Army: a woman was dying with her hands and feet nailed into the floor of the barrack where other women, who seemed not to see her at all, drifted by.

They change bulbs, clean away excrement, dress wounds occasionally, very occasionally, bring morphine, everything in five minutes, they don't have time to do more, they act frantically, but are perfectly well organized.

Hurbinek's hoarse groans arouse an ambivalent sense of tenderness, disgust and sorrow. They observe him in the darkness as they change the bulb yet again. One day they will be mothers. How horrible it would be if that child were their son. And yet they would love him.

The wheel of life continues to turn and they don't want to get left behind, they don't just want to remember the naked skulls, femurs and vertebrae visible under the skin on those bunks or in the mass graves where they are still burying the dead. They are young and they like Henek.

11

Henek never gets nervous. He is immutable. He does things calmly, as if he is applying a method. He never becomes impatient or irritated.

Nothing ever works out with Hurbinek and he always has to start from scratch. He doesn't swallow food and spits out water; he cleans his ass, then he shits himself again; he teaches him a word, and Hurbinek doesn't speak it.

Henek is tireless.

He takes him gingerly in his arms and on to the esplanade so he can feel the fresh air. The air inside is putrid. He walks around the shack with him, but it is freezing cold and Hurbinek's breathing immediately breaks into a gasping rattle; his body is about to fall apart and he has to bring him back inside. He very gingerly puts him back in the cradle he has made for him. For Henek, his weight is nearly unnoticeably light.

How could someone so fragile survive like that for three years? I wonder now in Frankfurt. That idea begins to torture me.

Henek isn't upset by Hurbinek's sad, forlorn gaze. He ignores it. Nothing about him disgusts him. He cleans out his ears when they are full of pus; he cleans his legs when he pees on himself; he cleans his tears away when he cries. He cries through open eyes.

12

Suddenly, one day, Hurbinek said something: some people heard *massklo*, others *matisklo*. It wasn't Hungarian; it was none of the words Henek had been trying to teach him. Nobody ever discovered what that word meant. Perhaps it was his real name.

13

Primo Levi writes, "Hurbinek, who had fought like a man, to the last breath, to gain his entry into the world of men, from which a bestial power had excluded him, died in the first days of March 1945, free but not redeemed."

When on that day, March 3, 1945, did Henek wake up and go to see Hurbinek?

When on that day, on that morning, did he realize that the shivers and panting had ceased?

When on that morning did he see that Hurbinek's eyes and mouth stayed open?

When in the night, did Hurbinek's heart stop, all by itself?

Nobody knew. With great integrity, after giving a deep sigh, Henek shut first the child's eyes and then his mouth. It was an astoundingly simple gesture. A gesture that was very common at the time, that even became trite and everyday; but all the same nothing could take away its solemnity, even in that factory of death.

Hurbinek's face was still warm. Henek covered him with a blanket. Helped by Primo Levi and Rubem Yetzev, he carried the cradle outside. The three waited four hours until other men came and put him in a barrow to take him to the mass grave. But Henek didn't want him to be buried there. Yetzev and he dug a hole at the foot of a tree, outside the precinct of the Main Camp, and there they lay little Hurbinek, swaddled in a blanket.

"Dear children, this Christmas I love you more than ever, but I must continue with my work for the sake of you and your happiness. This is my present," *SS Obergruppenführer* Heinz Rügen had written to his children on Christmas Eve.

III

THE TATTOO THAT WAS FORGOTTEN
OVER TIME

1

One day in 1917, it doesn't matter which, Cesare Levi, who was thirty-nine at the time, a good-looking, lively engineer with conservative political views, married Ester Luzzati in Turin, a twenty-two-year-old beautiful, imaginative girl who collected prints of natural life.

They were both Jews and descendents of Hebrews from Provence who in turn descended from the Sephardites expelled from Spain in 1492. They were married by Rabbi Mordecai Toledano, though neither was religious.

An electronics engineer like his father, Cesare was well established socially and belonged to the most influential circles in Piedmont thanks to his well-earned reputation. Levi the engineer enjoyed both professional and financial success in the demanding city on the Po, something that translated into his rapid promotion in markedly anti-Communist entrepreneurial circles.

When Mussolini's fascists appeared, he greeted them with ingenuous enthusiasm, and he even donned a black shirt at a few public events, though only a few.

2

On April 11, 1987 Primo Levi went out into the street for the last time. He had gotten up before dawn; it was still nighttime. A nightmare had prevented him from sleeping. Just another one of his usual nightmares. It was then, still in bed, that he took his decision, in that same bedroom where he had slept as a child. He decided to take his own life, to end things, to inscribe the fullstop. He was an old man, had experienced everything a human being could live and felt unnecessary. He had experienced too much.

He looked out of the window at the street; it was no longer raining as it had rained the previous evening. His nightmare was connected to the rain and long hours standing and being counted in the Buna-Monowitz camp under freezing rain that soaked you down to your bones and hit your head until it produced the terribly sharp headache he had never been able to throw off in all those years. That was why he had become addicted to umbrellas. He always carried one when he went out into the street.

In his nightmare, he was stuck under driving rain with his feet buried in mud, unable to move or lift himself. It wasn't yet another image he had dreamt up. Primo Levi remembered seeing an old French rabbi they had buried knee deep, whom they had stripped, whose *yarmulke* they stuffed into his mouth and whom they left for three days on the camp esplanade exposed to the snow and the gusts, until he died.

After he'd gotten dressed, Primo Levi walked falteringly down the passageway in his house where he lived with his wife Lucia and his senile mother and blind mother-in-law, both in their nineties and paralytic. He was very depressed, more than ever perhaps, and was worried by his prostate cancer. He no longer loved living, and wondered where he would find new reasons to make him love life anew.

He moved gracefully, accustomed to shadows and darkness. He was surprised that the decision to take his life, he, a man who had looked death in the face long ago and had never been able to drive its specter away, didn't seem at all dramatic, but logical, even happy, or perhaps merely the product of inertia.

He started thinking about how to do so in the old kitchen, employing the usual calculated intensity and methodical application he brought to the laboratory experiments he undertook in the course of his work.

He left the house because after his death, life would have to continue just as normal and he didn't want to leave any loose ends. He had an errand. He walked down several streets from Corso Re Umberto, in the Crocetta, and turned right into the fourth where he crossed and walked through a large entrance that led to a small courtyard, where Ugo Raboni, the photographer, had his shop.

He stopped when he saw it was shut. It was early, but he had anticipated that nobody would be there, and pushed an envelope under the door which contained instructions and several ten thousand lira bills.

The instructions referred to the fact that the photographer, his only friend from adolescence, should keep a large portait of his mother Esther that Raboni had taken on her fiftieth birthday and that a month before he had asked the same photographer to frame. What was that photo of his mother like, his beloved mother, who'd been in his mind at every moment in his life, who harrowed him now she'd become such a crazy old despot? What was his mother like before, his sweet, courageous and sensitive mother? In that dark alleyway, in the rain, on the last day of his life, Primo Levi could not recall his mother's face when she was young. For him she was the premonition that preceeds real, definitive death.

3

On July 31, 1919, Ester Luzzati de Levi was in labor and gave birth to a son. They called him Primo.

Primo's childhood was always marked by ill health and his mother's care, since the Levi family lived in fear of tuberculosis, pneumonia or whooping cough, illnesses that had led to the deaths of friends and relatives.

Ester spent many nights at the foot of her son's bed, reading books about science and zoology, her main interests. Primo Levi inherited her great curiosity about nature, particularly about fish.

For his sixth birthday, his mother gave him a large aquarium, the bottom of which was made of shards of lapislazuli. The red and silvery fish glowed in the water thanks to an electric device his father Cesare had installed at the back of the tank.

Years later he would remember how, on a whim, he'd called each fish after a mineral.

4

That present filled little Primo Levi with wonder and he always kept it near him like the lost treasure of innocence he would never again meet in the time he was forced to live.

Included in the instructions he listed in the letter he slipped under the door of Ugo Raboni's photography shop was one to the effect that the aquarium, now kept in his library—the same aquarium his mother gave him as a present on his sixth birthday—be given to Raboni himself on the day they got over the upset caused by their shock at his death, and executed the requisite legal measures.

The photo of his mother and the aquarium were the obejcts he loved most. He wasn't bothered about the fate of his other belongings and left no written wishes. They would remain with the family and his children Renzo and Lisa should decide what to do with his legacy.

5

At the age of fifteen, on his own initiative, young Levi enrolled in the Massimo D'Azeglio Grammar School where some of the leading intellectual opponents of

Mussolini's fascism were on the teaching staff. The school was renowned for its liberal approach. His father, currently under the influence of Lombroso's spiritualism, opposed his choice, but not too strenuously. Ester effortlessly brought him round.

It was in the Massimo D'Azeglio that he met Raboni and they enrolled together in Turin University in 1937. Both friends opted for Chemistry. Primo did so on the advice of his mother. He chose that subject because, together with Biology, it was what had most attracted him as an adolescent and where he had shown a leaning and some talent, given the lay, scientific spirit that informed the Levi household, not to mention the interests inculcated by his mother.

A year later, in October 1938, Benito Mussolini passed the Italian racial laws in Italy that decreed that no Jew could study or derive benefit from any of the advantages offered by the State. Nonetheless, Primo Levi continued his studies because he had entered the university the year before those segregationist laws were enacted. Even so, when he finished his degree with the highest possible marks in 1941, he was horrified to see that his degree certificate specified that the graduate belonged to the Hebrew race.

As a result he could find work nowhere, a situation he thought to be absurd and unjust. A year later, in 1942, after his father died of stomach cancer, he was offered an opening by Wander, a pharmaceutical company based in Milan and a branch of the Swiss Nestlé company. He grasped the opportunity and went to live in the rich city that was a rival to Turin. It was his first important journey, his first adventure in life.

I shall now follow the thoughts of Primo Levi. He left the sidestreet where his photographer friend owned a shop. He walked on until he reached the Via Roma. There he entered the Café San Carlo where he ordered a coffee made with cold milk. He'd not drunk anything at home, in the old family kitchen.

He proceeded to kill time until he could cross the road and go to the Barichelo laundry, by the Via Pietro Micca, where he collected his suits every week. Today was the day. Life will carry on, he thought yet again, and that encouraged him to see to that little errand and leave nothing undone, however small.

From where he sat, conscious it was the last time he would do so, in one direction he could see the Duomo and Piazza Castello. At the other end of that cloistered avenue stood the iron arches of the huge Porta Nuova Station. A station to which he had returned from hell on October 19, 1945.

While he drank his coffee and warmed up, he once again heard his mother's voice talking to him about chemists and naturalists and the great sea voyages of the eighteenth century, sailed by Bougainville, La Condamine and Cook, and recalled how she did so sitting in her armchair and holding a book.

He remembered the time when, as a child, she told him about the periodic table, as if it were a story, and about the man who formulated its laws in 1869, the Russian Mendeleev. He remembered that his mother told him another chemist, a German, Lothar Meyer, had argued that it was his discovery, and that his mother, when telling Meyer's story, adopted a gloomy, scornful tone, as a result of which, though he'd not really understood what his mother was saying, he immediately took the Russian's side, even if he'd been a callous killer.

Now, that morning, the words that fascinated him echoed round his head again, words like beryllium, fluorine, carbon, aluminium, phosphorus, potassium, scandium, titanium, vanadium, cobalt, arsenic, selenium, zirconium, niobium, palladium, tellurium, wolframium, bismuth, americium and so many others. Alone at the bar in the Café San Carlos he repeated them to himself mentally.

He could repeat straight off the periodic table with its one hundred and fifty elements. When he was a little boy, he found some of the valencies in that system highly amusing, like the ones for sodium (Na), hydrogen (H), magnesium (Mg), sulphur (S), iron (Fe), silver (Ag) or mercury (Hg). He also repeated these to himself mentally.

Ester, his mother, talked to him about concepts such as atomic mass, periods or noble gases: helium, neon, argon, krypton, xenon and radon.

This time out loud, and overheard by the waiter who didn't understand what Primo Levi—that old man leaning on the bar—was talking about as he absentmindedly looked out at the avenue, he repeated those words that sounded like a prayer or a wizard's ancient magic formula: helium-neon-argon-krypton-xenon and radon.

And he thought about something that he had remembered several years after surviving Auschwitz, he thought about the time when he arrived in Buna-Monowitz, where he was to be locked up as a slave, saw the layout of the barracks, and told the person next to him that it looked like the grid of the periodic table: the so-called *periods* in horizontal rows and the so-called *groups* in vertical columns.

Once again he brought back to his memory that Lothar Meyer, a German, and perhaps a good man, whom he and his mother found so unpleasant, vying with poor Mendeleev, about whom he knew nothing, except that either in reality or in his imagination, though he couldn't say why, he fell victim to the German. That was the real law of the periodic table, he finally remembered ironically: to be a victim of a German; and new concepts of chemistry were established in Auschwitz: mass fear, techniques of torture, valencies for annihilation, atoms of invisibility, formulas for extermination, fusion by cremation.

7

Primo Levi joined the anti-fascist resistance movement "Justice and Freedom," perhaps to reject the fascist policies his father didn't condemn even when he could see that Jews were being compelled to stay in their ghettos and their civil and labor rights were restricted, or perhaps simply as an outright rejection of his father's indulgent attitude toward the regime. He fled to the mountains to join the partisans, though he knew nothing about military strategy and the use of arms. That happened in 1943, shortly after the fall of Mussolini and the inception of the Republic of Salò.

He was with his comrades Maestro and Nissim in the Aosta Valley when he was captured by fascist militia on December 13, 1943 in a retaliation attack that caught the group unaware. He was taken to the Carpi-Fossoli concentration camp, where he was identified as a Jew in addition to being a partisan, thus aggravating his position.

8

Three months later he left in a German goods train comprising twelve cattle trucks packed with 650 Italian Jews.

Its final destination was a place in Poland called Auschwitz that he and those men, women and children had never heard of before. "A name without significance for us at the time," he was to write years later in *If This Is a Man*, "but it at least implied some place on this earth."

When the war ended, only 23 returned to Italy from the 650 people that formed that sinister convoy at dawn of February 22, 1944. One of those 23 individuals was Primo Levi. All the rest died.

He reached Auschwitz on February 26. He survived the first selection by the train, when they took aside those who were to be sent straight to the gas chambers. They gassed no less than 536 of the 650 the minute they reached the camp.

He was tatooed with the number 174517.

He worked as a Nazi slave in the Buna-Monowitz camp next to Auschwitz. Buna-Monowitz was an industrial plant built by the powerful pharmaceutical firm IG Farben for the purpose of manufacturing synthetic fuels. Six miles from Auschwitz, Monowitz was a kind of gray, desolate city where they gathered every kind of prisoner: English, Ukranian, French and many others to a total of ten thousand. There were also German civilian engineers. "We are the slaves of the slaves who everyone can order around" he later wrote.

IG Farben also manufactured Zyklon B, the gas that was used in the extermination chambers, an invention of Rudolf Höss, one of the Auschwitz commandants.

Being a slave meant working twelve to fifteen hours with hardly any food or clothes, all to the profit of the Reich and, above all, of IG Farben.

Being a slave meant working until you were exhausted, until you were dead.

Being a slave meant making a profit from death; buying the deaths of others for free.

Being a slave meant you were nobody, were the object of all the manias, perversions and whims of the German SS. A slave had been shot down when he left the building where he worked simply because two German soldiers had laid a bet about who had the best aim. Another slave who wasn't working sufficiently hard was tied up a few inches from a jug of water and left to die of thirst. They changed the water everyday in front of him.

9

The Russian Red Army liberated the camp of Auschwitz Birkenau in January 1945. Primo Levi then began the long journey home that took him through Poland, Russia, Romania, Czechoslovakia, Austria, Germany, Switzerland and finally Italy. By the time he reached his home in Turin, the same house where he was born, it was already October.

He spent the rest of his life—thirty years—working as a chemist who specialized in synthetic varnishes. He sometimes worked as a translator. He wrote articles and gave lectures. Life after slavery wasn't easy.

He published books and won prizes.

His was a strange death.

10

He committed suicide on April 11, 1987 by throwing himself down the stairwell in the narrow space left by the lift. It happened like this.

He had walked back from the Barichelo laundry carefully carrying a clean gray suit wrapped in brown paper on a coat hanger.

He had taken a detour on his way home, and lingeringly walked down as far as the Piazza Bononi and Academia Albertina to take a final look at the Balbo gardens.

He asked the concierge, Jolanda Gasperi, for the post, but she didn't have it at hand.

He walked up the stairs to the third floor, actually the fourth, very slowly. An hour later he opened the door and threw himself down those same stairs as if he were diving headfirst into the cold waters of a river. Perhaps during the very last second, that is what he believed, that he was throwing himself into the cold waters of the Po.

Others say it was an accident: a particular medication he was taking made him dizzy and one dizzy spell caused him to fall over the banister. The fact is that Mrs. Gasperi, the concierge, who had taken up the mail he'd wanted only a few minutes before, hadn't noticed anything strange in his attitude, no expression of anguish that was any worse than normal, and no somber tone in his voice. He had thoughtfully thanked her, as he always did.

He had always been a discreet, taciturn man, though on occasions he could be full of vitality. He preferred to pass unnoticed, but life had ceased to have any meaning forty years earlier, when he watched how Henek placed the final spadefuls of earth over the small grave where the remains of Hurbinek lay.

He sometimes convinced himself that those who had died there were better than the survivors. It wasn't easy to overcome that perverted guilt, the guilt of having saved oneself.

Those who knew him well know that he was often tortured by the thought that he had forgotten the number tattooed on Hurbinek's arm. That was his worst slavery, together with the slavery of having survived. He had memorized the number and then over time forgotten it, despite himself. It would have been a useless, shaming memory, but one that was necessary.

53

IV

SIGNS OF LIFE IN THE DISTANCE

1

Chocolate

1936. Nine years before Hurbinek's death.

Before entering the living room where all her family is waiting, Sofia Cèrmik adjusts her new tulle dress in a dark, neat and tidy bedroom that looks over Targova Street, the most commercial street in the city of Rzeszów, in the Carpathians of Upper Galicia.

Gathered there already are Raca her mother, Simon her father and Uncle and Aunt Pitlik and the Vigos, her single aunts, Sara and Mikaela, her elder brothers, Max and Aaron and the young Stefan and Anna. Friends and customers of her father also visit the house and bring small token presents. They are all happy and are all going to celebrate her birthday with her. She is sixteen.

She is young and beautiful with a bright, cheerful face, and to that day she has lived without worrying about what is happening beyond the Vistula and the San and its small tributary the Wislok that flows very close to their house, very close to Simon Cèrmik and his partner, Uncle Gork Vigo's salted fish and meat and spice store, beyond the wooded Carpathians and beyond the great city of Krakow, where she has never set foot and whose bookshops she dreams about.

When she emerges from the small bedroom in the new tulle dress that is her mother's present, she is greeted by a loud burst of applause in the dining room and hallway. The hurrays ring out like the green branches of trees lashing a tanned hide.

All the family relatives start to kiss Sofia, as do neighbors who keep coming and her girl friends from school, and suddenly a luminous party atmosphere spreads throughout the Cèrmik household.

It was a special Spring day.

The china cups are brimming with hot chocolate and they eat sponge cakes baked by Raca.

It's five o'clock in the afternoon and a guitar strikes up a romantic song that speaks of love and travel.

Gradually, chocolate splashes every face, moustache and beard, and the women's red lips and children's pale cheeks. The dogs of the house lick up the leftovers on the plates in the kitchen.

There are garlands and flowers in every corner of the living room held up with the many books in the house. Shopkeeper Cèrmik brings out bottles of anisette and other liqueurs he offers to his guests. His eyes ooze with satisfaction behind his glasses.

Simon Cèrmik makes a toast to his favorite daughter who sips on her glass, glowing and blushing.

Sofia is slim, but her shape is subtle, firm and well defined. Just a few months ago she abandoned the last traces of herself as a little girl and changed into a woman with a slender waist and broad hips. Her skin is smooth and her hair fair, fragrant and very curly. Her voice, sweet, low and enveloping.

Yakov, the son of the Pawlickas, the schoolteachers, has come to the birthday party and can't take his eyes off her. Although she is rather taken aback, Sofia returns his look and offers him a cup of hot chocolate.

They have known each other forever but it is the first time they have looked at each other like that. Tall as houses, dreams are sometimes real and can be reached like the stars, Sofia thinks as she watches Yakov and feels her fingers brush his as they have never done before. Or are the stars dreams? People in Rzeszów are still not sure. Some went on singing deep into the night.

2

Portrait

1945. Seven months after Hurbinek's death.

Targova Street in Rzeszów has hardly changed in these years of war. The shops are the same, although they have lost the color they had and it has been a long time since they sold anything new or truly useful.

Targova Street, the old business hub in the small city, is now swept by gusts of wind that blow up clouds of dust that were never so thick in the pre-war years.

Grandmother Raca Cèrmik, Zelman by her maiden name, stares through the window at that end-of-autumn wind. Russian troops had knocked on her door yet again asking her for milk and meat, but the houses have no cows, hens or rabbits. The gardens bear sparse produce that soon rots. Raca gave the three baby-faced soldiers a couple of fresh turnips and a head of garlic.

They have taken all the wine and spirits that were in the cellar, the old bottles kept there for big occasions by her husband Simon Cèrmik, felled by a heart attack on that same Targova Street, in 1942, when a German soldier forced him to run from one end of the street to the other carrying a large drum of gasoline. As he lay on the sidewalk, the German poured it over him and set fire to him, but old Cèrmik was already dead.

Raca stands and looks out of the window after the Russian soldiers have gone, but she's not really looking at the wind, however much the wind puts on a show, blowing away paper, leaves and clothes from washing lines.

Raca sees another street in other times.

She sees that distant morning when Sofia was five years old and a man crossed Targova Street in a very determined fashion, knocked on their door and asked for the girl.

It was a Norwegian painter, though he looked more like a homeless man. His name was Gottwold, he was very tall and an inevitable sadness dwelled on his bearded, lean face. He had noticed Sofia when she was playing in the entrance to the Cèrmik store. He simply wanted to draw a portrait of her.

Raca opened the door, and asked Gottwold in after he had told her what he wanted to do. He had come from

Katowice, where he knew his sister was married to a Pole by the name of Dayna, but when he got there, he discovered this Dayna, whom he did not know personally, had killed his young wife and their two children and had then taken his own life. Devastated by the news of that tragedy, Gottwold wept for his sister for some time but then, rather than returning to Norway, where no one was waiting for him, he stayed in the district tramping around like a surly gypsy shunning the presence of human beings. He painted whatever he felt like. He'd been doing that for three years and his backpack was stuffed with paper and cardboard covered in drawings. He had recently been wandering around Mielec and Kolbuszowa, where Raca came from, very near Rzeszów, and perhaps that was why Sofia's mother decided to give him lodging for a time.

A few days later Gottwold painted Sofia.

Now as Raca looks out of the window and remembers that man coming, the Cèrmik house is desolate and cold because she has lived there alone ever since the Germans took her family away. Raca doesn't try to clean or keep it warm. Nor are there many photos or portraits left on the walls or cupboards, although she does have lots of memories. They pass through her mind time and again as she waits for insanity to sweep here into these memories and save her from this world.

The portrait that the sad, silent Norwegian drew of Sofia hangs in a prominent position in her bedroom. When she looks at it, for a few seconds Raca thinks that bright-eyed girl will run into the house at any moment, terrified by one of those vague, frightening things that scare children but are only fantasy stoked by non-existent horrors. Then the immense, infinite love that Raca has always possesed slips out of her hands.

3

Wedding

1941. Four years before Hurbinek's death.

There is a lot of fear in Rzeszów on the day when Sofia Cèrmik and Yakov Pawlicka get married. In recent weeks there have been massacres of Jews carried out by the *Einsatzkommandos*—the SS police batallions—in the small towns close to Debica, only twelve miles to their west, and Przeworsk, further east and near the frontier. Nobody, it seems, did anything to prevent them.

Sofia and Yakov decided they wanted to marry before they met the fate destiny held in store.

Yakov is a mechanic and knife grinder. He looks sturdy, although he is short, and bald and stubborn when it comes to getting what he wants. He had taken over the business after his mother's eccentric brother, Elias Papoulk, hung himself from the branch of a tree in the birch forest you can make out from Sofia's bedroom, on the far bank of the Wislok. Elias Papoulk had died a childless bachelor, and Yakov had been working as an apprentice for him.

Yakov has loved Sofia and Sofia has loved Yakov ever since they were adolescents. They have pledged to live happily, "come what may." They will work together. They will protect each other from all evil. They swear that under the *chuppah*, the wedding canopy. "You will listen to me."

"I will listen to you." "You will take my hand." "I will take your hand."

After their wedding, they go to live in the same house where the unfortunate Elias lived when he was alive. He had secretly bequeathed it to his nephew before committing suicide. Apart from a workshop with all the tools a mechanic needs, there are around a hundred hens, enough to make a little business from the sale of eggs. "If those German dogs don't make their lives impossible," comments Rachel, Yakov's mother, when someone rhetorically asks about the young couple's future.

It is an austere wedding: there is hardly any wine although they do have beer and the local mead that is brown and sweet. It is held at the Pawlickas' house because the Cèrmik's house has been flooded by the swollen waters of the River Wislok. "Don't worry about the dowry," Simon Cèrmik tells prospective father-in-law Samuel Pawlicka. "My daughter's money didn't get soaked." "It's not your money that will make my Yakov happy." "No, it won't be the money." "He and the lot of us will be happy if those dogs forget us." "May God will that." "May He indeed." Samuel repeats wearily as he looks up at the sky.

While the two men talk, Yakov has started to sing. He sings very well, everybody agrees, his is a powerful, melodious voice. His best friend, Pavel Ramadian, a mustachioed joker from Armenia who came to Rzeszów with his parents to work in the Carpathian woodmills accompanies him on the violin.

Sofia is proud and blushes when Yakov sings. The song he sings speaks of a falcon that flies alone until it falls in love with a pigeon, but the pigeon is afraid and flies far away so the falcon can't reach her.

Then Pavel sings an impish song to make the women laugh.

There aren't many guests at the wedding because nobody in the town is in a mood to celebrate. It is not a wedding full of happiness yet there is laughter and a will to live. They all congratulate and hug each other as if wanting to keep at bay the ill omens that give them sleepless nights, and congratulate the families of bride and groom and wish the couple a long life and healthy children who can pray for them when it is time to die.

Few people are actually there, not because the Cèrmiks and Pawlickas are not much loved in Rzeszów—they are families the community appreciates highly—but because over the last year many neighbors have begun to flee further south with all their belongings, toward the Danube, Bulgaria and Greece, and from there to Palestine. Few people attend because few have stayed on.

But those who do come to Sofia and Yakov's wedding do so to feel they are leading normal lives with their friends, if possible for one last time. They eat with relish the geese reared by Raca and her single sisters. They dig into the tender flesh of roast kid, and trays of aromatic black pudding and devour the desserts— figs with honey, clusters of walnuts and blackcurrants in bittersweet sauce.

They eat to drive away thoughts of when the plague will reach their door. They eat in silence. A silence broken by Yakov's songs and Pavel's sad music, Pavel who is drunk and sobbing. "It's the bride. She is young and beautiful."

Pavel suddenly climbs onto a chair, and tells the children who are making such a din on tables at the back to be quiet, and offers a solemnly worded toast to the newlyweds. It is a long, poetic toast and he asks them to celebrate this wedding every ten years, all together in bigger and bigger parties. "So that the house may prosper and our souls as well."

They all raise their glasses but their skin looks gray. Their faces and hands are gray. The smoke from cigarettes and pipes wreathes their faces and makes the gray even grayer.

Yakov kisses Sofia on the lips. Then he puts his mouth close to her ear. The exhausted guests applaud politely. "We will have lots of children and I will love you for a hundred years." "Yakov, Yakov, I'm sorry, forgive me." "Why do you say that you are sorry, why do you ask me to forgive you?" "Because I won't live so long." "Oh, yes, you will. Somewhere you will live with me."

4

Thunder

1965. Twenty years after Hurbinek's death.

Cousin Moritz Pawlicka listens attentively, as he waits on the sidewalk of New York's Fifth Avenue, to the words being broadcast from the radio of a taxi parked by a fire hydrant. They sound like words recited in Hebrew. He is on his way to work at a newspaper, the *New York Post*, but stopped to listen to those words because he has suddenly been stirred by a memory from his childhood: he is a child, is in his native Poland with his whole family seated behind the desks in Grandfather Samuel's school while a storm rages outside. The claps of thunder make the glass panes vibrate. Moritz keeps his fear to himself and pretends, or better still, Ira his father soothes him by affectionately caressing the back of his neck. He gives one hand to his father while the other plays with a button on Uncle Yakov's jacket. His brand new Aunt Sofia is leaning on Yakov and smoothing his hair sweetly with her hand. It is *Passover* and they are all listening to the patriarch Samuel Pawlicka reading the *Haggadah* in his grave, firm voice, though Moritz notices that now and then they try to look out of the corners of their eyes into the street. The diaphanous air seems unthreatening and the clouds he cannot see are turning yellow in the distance. Moritz will never forget that afternoon when he heard the story of the exodus of the Jews to Egypt, although he had heard his grandfather tell that story many times before, because the thunderclaps weren't coming from the sky but from German canons.

5

Letters

1912. Thirty three years before Hurbinek's death.
  Thomas Zelman is writing a letter to his elder sister, Raca. He is in the English port of Southampton and has embarked on a fashionable liner and it is a rainy day

in April. They will set sail in a few hours and Thomas writes under a canopy on the fourth deck, surrounded by people bawling their goodbyes. He is telling Raca in his letter that he has found work in Boston, in the house of relatives who left Rzeszów at the end of the nineteenth century and set up home in America. He will work as a milliner like them. Those same relatives who will welcome him sent him money to purchase a third-class passage on a giant boat that all the newspapers have featured, the *Titanic*. Thomas Zelman is twenty years old, impulsive and happy. He sends kisses to all the family in his letter. "They will soon be dollar bills," he says. April 14 is his birthday and he asks Raca to think of him on that day. He will be on the high seas and will do what he can to have a bottle to uncork. He wonders at the end of his letter whether he will get very seasick on the boat. He has never been on board one. However, a new life awaits him. The century promises much and he feels rumbustiously alive as if he were on a never-ending binge. He seals the envelope and is about to go on land to take the letter to a post office but it is too late. Night is falling and they have removed the gangplanks and the bands are competing with the din of the horns and howls of passengers under the shower of confetti falling from the main decks. He re-opens the envelope and adds a PS in which he pledges to his sister that he will write to her daily on the boat and will send her all the letters together from America as soon as they reach port.

Thomas Zelman was unable to do that; he froze to death in the sea, on the night of his birthday.

Raca was not to not hear anything about the fate of her brother for a year. She never received letters from him nor imagined that they existed. One day Sofia told Yakov the story of her uncle who went down with the *Titanic*. She did so when she noticed her fiancé watching when Raca opened a drawer in the sideboard and took out a photo she kissed three times slowly. It was the photo of Thomas her brother that she raised to her lips every night before she went to bed. Nobody ever found out about the letters, and in conversations they mentioned the "American" uncle who died in the middle of the ocean as if it were a fabled story or an unreal, mythical event magnified by the provincial atmosphere in that small community of Rzeszów. For Sofia, imagining her uncle caught by chance in that shipwreck, embellished by the drawings in the magazines that reached their shop thanks to the spice suppliers from Krakow, was as fascinating as a novel, like the *Madame Bovary* she found so absorbing, or so many books she devoured by herself. Even Simon Cèrmik—who always a skeptic—would finish smoking his cigar talking about his brother-in-law as if he were the hero in an adventure story, whose deeds he exaggerated, but Raca left the room when her husband fantasized over that misfortune. "Don't allow them to destroy your memory of me," she heard her brother's voice say inside her head. And she cherished that strange private space where only the ghost of Thomas Zelman was present.

6

Books

1932. Thirteen years before Hurbinek's death.

The adolescent Yakov Pawlicka finishes his apprentice's work in the afternoon in Uncle Elias Papoulk's knife-grinding workshop and relishes the reading of stories of Sinbad the Sailor in a volume with thick battered covers. It is the only book in the workshop and the only book old Elias has ever read. "Don't do as I do," he tells his nephew, whom he sees open the book immediately once he has washed his hands after putting the tools away.

The truth is that young Yakov does read more books, as many as he can from the ones his parents keep in their dining room. "I read more books, but this is my favorite." "How many books can you read in your life?" "I don't know, thousands and thousands." "Will you have the time, with all the work there is to do?" "I will do my work and read at night." "No, you won't, because you will have to look after your children, attend to your friends and love your wife." "I will find the time. I really will, Uncle Elias." "You will have to read in secret, but you won't have much time for your secrets, so you will read very few books." "I will read in secret." "What else will you do in secret?" "How can I know what life will bring? Can anyone ever know?" "No, of course not, but there will be secret things you do by yourself, with no one else around, like the worm that burrows into the ground. And life will bring you many secret moments, by yourself. What will you do then, read?" "I will read." "No, you won't, you will lament, you will lament the fact that you are alive, you will point your fist at the sky and will be unhappy. You will do what I did, when I was knocked over by a cart, when I was your age and I shut myself in my room to suffer the pain by myself, without anyone hearing or seeing, and when my injuries most hurt, I stretched out and waited for death to come, wished it would come. I went four days without eating or sleeping, the bones in my feet had been crushed. Yakov, never be alone. You will end up imagining things and seeing devils. You will sell your soul to one." "No, uncle, I won't do any of that. I will read, and will read lots of books." "I hope they let you, Yakoimele."

7

Jamaica

1935. Ten years before Hurbinek's death.

What can Yakov Pawlicka see hanging from a lamppost in Berlin? An ear. But can it be a *human ear* hanging from a lamppost in Berlin? It is the ear of a Jew. And how does he know? There is a card at the bottom of the post that says "Jew's ear = Pig's ear." They cut it off days ago and stuck it on a hook, then they attached the hook to a piece of string and threw it over the top of the lamp, where it hooked up.

It is the first thing Yakov sees when he leaves the station.

He has come to take a vacation in Berlin, where a German friend of his who was born in Rzeszów lives. His friend's name is Sigmund. Sigmund what? Yakov can't remember, or in fact doesn't know.

Jamaica is Yakov's dream. He tells Sigmund that in the Café Hannover. He has wanted to go to Jamaica ever since he saw a map of the island on an atlas that belonged to his parents, at school in Rzeszów. The name, Jamaica, seduced him. And the pirate stories his brothers David and Ira told him. He wants to go there in a sailing ship, sail around the island, anchor in Montego Bay, gaze at the horizon from the highest peaks of the Blue Mountains, sleep in Port of Spain.

Sigmund tells him to wake up, that dreams are not the most sensible things in present times, even less so for a Jew. But he doesn't say the word "Jew" in the café; it wouldn't be prudent. Instead he says "one of yours."

When he heard that, Yakov wondered how much of a friend that Sigmund whom he knew from school, but whose family never visited the Pawlicka household could ever be.

A demonstration suddenly erupts around a corner where there are public baths, between the avenue and the street with the Café Hannover terrace. People are carrying placards with stars of David and demanding justice.

Sigmund says it is all very well to have demonstrations like this, but they aren't realistic, and that one has to go with the flow of history.

The police gathers at the other end of the street and they charge on horseback. The police have swords and long leather nightsticks. The clash is brutal and people scatter everywhere. As they chase after the demonstrators, some police drive their horses into the straw chairs on the café terrace.

Yakov and Sigmund run to protect themselves from the blows the police are indiscriminately delivering to everyone. In the tumult, Yakov is suddenly surrounded by people running who drag him along as they flee in panic. He loses sight of Sigmund in the hysterical avalanche.

Eventually, in that labyrinth of streets, he finds he is alone with another young man of his age. They look at each other in fear, as they hear the sound of horse hoofs behind them, galloping over the street paving stones. Two mounted police approach, flourishing their swords.

The youth signals to Yakov, who follows unflinchingly, not sure what the next step will be. They enter a house whose sinister black door is open and climb the stairs to the first landing. The police rides in on horseback and up the stairs.

The young men are forced to go up to the top, to the fourth landing. The policeman reaches the third but his horse slips, takes fright and rears up, neighing and throwing off the policeman who tumbles down the stairs until he gets caught on a bend. As he falls his saber sticks into his left thigh and he lets out a loud howl. The horse continues its descent and tramples on its rider who writhes in pain.

As they watch the scene unfold, Yakov and his friend also rush downstairs. When he passes by the policeman, Yakov stops moved by fear and pity. His eyes seem to be calling out for help, but when he goes over, the policeman stretches his hand out to grab him by the arm. Yakov then sees hate in his eyes and two swastikas on the sleeves of his uniform.

Yakov manages to break away from the policeman. He is scared when he gets out into the street. He looks to his right and sees two other police on horseback savagely beating the young man who'd been accompanying him. Yakov flees in the opposite direction, but never sees another sign of Sigmund. Nor does he see him in his house when he rushes back to collect his luggage. That same night Yakov took the last train back to Poland.

Why Jamaica? Why those dreams? Does a place called Jamaica really exist? And why? They are questions to ponder in a train travelling across Europe, if you can't get to sleep.

Ice skating is his favorite sport, for example when the Wislok is frozen and as hard as stone. He's not sure why, but in that train that first takes him to Krakow and then, many hours later, to Rzeszów, Yakov can only think about two ideas that obsess him, opposed ideas that keep recurring: Jamaica and the frozen river in the city of his birth. "No, Jamaica doesn't exist, Sigmund, and if it did exist, it wouldn't serve any purpose," he would now tell that strange, perhaps cowardly Sigmund if he ever saw him again. But he never would.

8

Fruit

1925. Twenty years before Hurbinek's death.

Peaches, apples and wild strawberries in a basket at the feet of Sofia Cèrmik. She is surrounded by the loud voices of men who are strange but not hostile—one only has to see her mother's relaxed face.

She is barely five years old and her mother Raca takes her by the hand while the men continue filling the basket with the fruit from the piles on the stall.

Sofia has never seen fruit. It is something new for her, as to a certain extent is her awareness that it is midday, that the springtime light is darkened by the pollen and dust in the air and that the smell wafting her way is as much from the fresh vegetables as from the rotten. But it's a lot to ask of someone so young to distinguish between life and death.

The dense, golden sky is a warning that there will be storms in the afternoon, like yesterday. They will collect snails when it dries out, at sunset.

A man is sitting next to the stall with the peaches, apples and wild strawberries. He is holding a big wooden bucket between his legs. He keeps extracting prickly pears from a sack on the ground next to him. He picks them up very carefully so as not to prick himself on the spikes on their rough skin. Then he peels them with a knife and the moist, greeny fruit immediately appears. He places the peeled prickly pears in the wooden bucket. The man offers Sofia one. She hides behind her mother's skirt, but Raca taps her on the head authorizing her to take it. The fresh, sharp taste of a prickly pear in her mouth will be a pleasurable sensation that will accompany Sofia in her short life.

In Auschwitz the search for that sensation was often to come to her mind—a raging desire because she so misses that simple pleasure—but it was to be a memory that wouldn't find a way into that absurd horror. On the other hand she was to remember the morning when she acompanied her mother to the market and watched that man peeling prickly pears and how there was a fire near the esplanade full of peddlers, and black particles of soot started to fly through the air like a downpour of tiny pieces of coal.

Everyone runs to the pond to pump water, but Sofia only feels her mother's hand squeezing hers. "They look like little black flies," says Sofia referring to the wandering particles. "No, they are the ashes of the Synagogue, it's burning."

Sofia looks at the seven-year-old boy opposite who has just spoken to her. He is carrying a bag of juniper berries on his back and a basket in his hand where a cockerel is stretching its neck out of curiosity. "Do you remember me?" "Yes, you're Yakov Pawlicka. I sometimes see you through the window when your mother is cutting your hair," says Sofia as she strokes the cockerel's crest.

The two of them are older now than their son was to be when he died.

9

Souls

1960. Fifteen years after Hurbinek's death.

It is snowing. The tractors with their improvised scoops are clearing the snow off the paths so the cows can water and the few vehicles in town can circulate.

But Raca Cèrmik is averse to all that, or rather lives isolated from all that, because she can't forgive, or consent to life, or allow what she remembers to pass.

Raca Cèrmik, Zelman by her maiden name, is in her house in Rzeszów that looks over Targova Street, and is drinking her fourth cup of Turkish coffee of the day and smoking a long cigarette, and is looking back and wondering what became of her family.

What became of her little children whose photos in all sizes and frames fill the tables and shelves of her home?

What became of the soul of her cheerful, joking Aaron, who was always so mischievous, and dead aged twenty-six in Auschwitz?

What became of the soul of her impressionable, hard-working son Stefan, who was sickly and shy, and dead aged twenty-four in Auschwitz?

What became of the soul of her fragile, delicate daughter Sofia, her sweet, little Sofia, and dead aged twenty-three in Auschwitz?

And what might her elder children, Anna and Max, be doing, the survivors so far way, wherever they happen to be? They left this land and now write her letters and want her to go and live with them in a place called Detroit. But she won't go.

What became of the soul of her relative, elegant, strong-minded Samuel Pawlicka who died in Auschwitz?

What became of the souls of the children of Samuel, David and Yakov, good Yakov who loved Sofia. All dead in Auschwitz too?

What became of the soul of her friend Gork Vigo, and her sisters Sara and Mikaela Zelman, who all disappeared in the oven of some concentration camp?

Where did each and everyone of them end up? How did each and everyone die? Did each and everyone suffer as they died? Raca Cèrmik, Zelman by her maiden name, tortures herself alone.

But she will never wonder after the soul of Hurbinek, her grandchild, because she doesn't even know he existed. Life kept that hidden from her.

V

THE LONG JOURNEY FROM BLACK TO WHITE

1

I was going to Auschwitz, but not anymore.

Dr. Voghs touches my knees as he examines X-rays of my legs carefully against the light. The expression on his face beneath rimless spectacles is worrying because it is like the defensive smile of a second-hand car dealer.

Voghs is on in years, possibly approaching retirement. He has replaced the young, rosy-cheeked doctor I had when I was admitted who is doing his training here with a mixture of indifference and conviction. On the other hand, Voghs reminds me of that terrifying type of person who lives in terror and whose immediate physical peculiarity is never to look you in the eye as they tell you something drastic related to what remains of your life, such as "You've got cancer" or "You will be executed tomorrow" or "Your daughter has died" or "You will never walk again."

I have felt reduced to an object more than once in the Frankfurt Universitäts-Kliniken where I am hospitalized.

The nurses, naturally, do their best to create the very real impression that you are a nobody.

Like an old country doctor, Voghs forces me to move my toes that stick out beyond the plaster casts completely paralyzing my legs. For the third time over the last few days since my accident, he asks me if I was traveling through Germany as a tourist. It's become a routine, police kind of enquiry, "Going to Berlin, right?" he asks.

He thinks he is amusing. I think about what Joseph Roth said when the Nazis were ruling the roost in Germany with majority support. "Who in their right mind goes to Berlin of their free will?" Roth was referring to the *Ostjuden*, the Jews from the East, but I fear that his question, albeit a rhetorical one, still holds today.

I reply to Dr. Voghs that I was heading to Auschwitz. But not anymore. "To see the ossuaries?" he asks keeping his eyes firmly on my X-rays, though I surmise it's out of clumsy innocence. I reply, surprised and hesitant, that I don't know if there are ossuaries in Auschwitz. "I don't know either, it's what I've heard, I've never been," he continues as if that were an end to the matter.

"Of course," I recapitulated ironically, "what German ever goes to Auschwitz of his own free will?"

All the same I've never thought of ossuaries. Who ever thinks of ossuaries, like that, on the spur of the moment, without having a powerful reason to do so? Or, at the very least, who can ever think of ossuaries that aren't the ones you find at the scene of any battle in past centuries that has now been converted into some sort of theme park? Or in the most out-of-the-way churches in Castile or Sicily? Or in archaeological museums. "You think there might be ossuaries in Auschwitz?" I ask Voghs maliciously. My chest hurts when I breathe. "I thought the crematoria were working all the time and that's how they saved themselves the bother of piles of bones after they gassed people." "I don't know, it's what I've heard, one hears so many theories . . . " he says, still averting his gaze and taking on a condescending tone. He taps me on the knee and walks over to one of the other beds in the ward, still smiling cruelly behind his glasses.

I have seen the occasional ossuary and imagined that they are the remains of human beings waiting for an eventual onset of justice. Like in Ruanda. Like in Bosnia. Like in Cambodia. I expect those countries also have their Dr. Voghs. "Time inevitably brings about justice," the old drunkard Roth used to say. Sooner or later, it does. I really believe that. Does that make me naïve?

2

Those who came out of Auschwitz did so down to their bones. They were no more than bones. That was their only possession, the skeleton that had survived, their own personal ossuary. They returned emptied out, bewildered, with no moral horizon or bodily flesh, sparse guts too worn out to function, ravaged, tortured, wandering. No language could contain the brutal range of their experience.

But life went on. They traveled from black to white, returned to the opposite pole.

What did they do afterward? How did they live, how did they die? What did they feel as daily life brought forgetfulness to such a marred memory? And yet prior questions existed, the anwers to which were beyond the reach of those who survived Auschwitz: What became of their towns, their villages and their homes? Where were their families? Down to what kind of bones had their loved ones, their friends, their neighbors and their rivals come? Could you perhaps describe as normal the life you lived after the Red Army reached Auschwitz and liberated the camp? We don't know how many answers these questions might have been given, perhaps as many as there are survivors. But we *do* know that two million answers are eternally inaudible: the dead don't speak.

And Hurbinek?

What remained of Hurbinek in the memories of those who were present at his final agony in that infirmary improvised in the Main Camp?

Let us start with Henek.

We know that Henek was really Belo König—Primo Levi says that, when he relates how the Polish nurses who couldn't face looking after Hurbinek changed König to Henek—and how Belo König returned to northern Transylvania in July 1945. He joined the Hungarian army, where he displayed great courage in everything he did, being so full of life and energy. He forged a career and soon reached the rank of captain of the forces that confronted the Soviets in the streets of Budapest in 1956. Some thought Captain König was a hero. Others didn't.

He married Claricia Novaceanu, a Romanian national skating champion, and had three children. He never knew the youngest, Joanine: the day she came into the world, her father was executed in a prison in Minsk where they court-martialed the "traitors" behind that 1956 revolt. Those who had dealings with him always mentioned how he smiled broadly right to the end. He didn't have a last word to say. He uttered no farewells.

We know Claricia Novaceanu never heard him speak about the real Hurbinek. On the other hand, he did speak at length about the other people he met in Auschwitz (as was the case with an Italian chemist) and told terrible stories of what he had experienced there in a matter-of-fact tone. However, we don't know if he ever referred in public to the crippled child he had looked after with so much devoted care. He apparently didn't.

But Claricia Novaceanu did recall later, on the day her elder son Stanislazh was married in 1972, that Belo, alias Henek, used to tell Stanislazh, when he was very young, the story of a tree whose trunk housed a very pale being with the face and body of a little boy, a legless little boy. He had named this astonishing being Hurbinek and entitled the story "Hurbinek's tree." Claricia remembered it all of a sudden at the wedding; she remembered right there why that strange name was so unexpectedly familiar to her; she remembered it when her daughter-in-law asked her about Stanislazh's childhood with the curiosity of someone who was in love.

It was a story her husband told time and again with slight variations, but always with the same conclusion: the unhappy, tiny inhabitant of that tree couldn't get out because he had no legs, he wept inside the tree and, if you listened carefully, pressed your ear against the trunks of those trees, you could hear him moaning or gasping. That was why Claricia remembered how her children, when they were very young, would go from tree to tree, put their little faces next to the trunks and try to hear a voice, while Belo told them, "Listen hard, very hard and you will hear him. He sometimes says my name. He sometimes calls out to me." And Stanislazh or his brother Josef would get very excited and suddenly shout "Yes, yes, he said Henek, he said Henek!"

Claricia remembered it then, as if it were a sudden revelation. But she didn't know the source of that story, just as she didn't know that a tree that held Hurbinek's spirit within it grew in a place in Poland that the Germans once called Auschwitz.

3

Rubem never forgot the day when, with Levi and Henek, he buried Hurbinek's small body at the foot of a tree. When he returned to Radzyn, his birthplace, the Hebrew schools where he taught weren't there any more and he managed to find a job as a postman working for the Polish Post Office. He wept a lot, disconsolately, when he found out that what he had so feared was true: that his wife, Demetria, was gassed that same night they had reached Auschwitz and had been separated on the platform when one of the guards' mastiffs bit her.

He had to undergo psychiatric treatment for years because he suffered from nightmares and woke up soaked in sweat and dirtied by his own defecations. They were dreams prompted by pure fear, the doctors told him. Yetzev would relate his dream, that was invariably the same: he could see the man right in front of him in a long queue changing into a tobacco pouch made from his own skin. Several SS tortured him until they broke him. The torturers' words were broadcast round the camp from a loudspeaker: "If you don't help us, it will hurt a lot." And those final words would hang in the air: "hurt a lot . . . hurt a lot . . . " A screaming voice drilled through his eardrum and Yetzev also shouted out, *Jawohl, jawohl!* When he woke up, he confirmed night after night that he no longer controlled his sphincters and had shit himself in bed.

A year before he died, in 1965, Rubem Yetzev decided to return to Auschwitz and seek out the tree beneath which Hurbinek was buried. He found it, or thought he had. He told the person accompanying him, someone much younger than himself: "Not a single day goes by when I don't think about the child we buried by the foot of this tree. He has lived in my memory to this day." The tree, a huge acacia, was very leafy and now brought shade to an irregularly shaped esplanade where Oven no. 2 had stood before it was blown up.

Old Yetzev stood there for a whole afternoon and stared at the capricious shape of the roots that stuck out. As he pictured Hurbinek's fragile, pathetic body yet again, he tried unsuccessfully to chase from his head the memory of the earth that shifted in the covered graves where they executed and threw thousands of wounded Jews in Radzyn. He had seen that earth billow by itself as the bodies buried on top of each other swelled up.

4

We know that Ernst Sterman, a German Jew, a china manufacturer, visited high mountain spas and health establishments throughout the United States, where he went in 1946 to cure himself from the aftermath of the tuberculosis he contracted in the final months of his incarceration in Auschwitz. He was spared from one of the fatal "selections" because of a mere arithmetical error on the part of his guards. When it was time to count the bodies that were shaking with fear when they were about to enter the gas chamber though he hadn't stripped naked like the others yet, a punctilious bureaucrat sent him back to the barrack. There was one too many, and chance meant it was him. He was hidden there for two months and contracted tuberculosis. He lost one lung and more than half the capacity of the other.

He disappears in 1955 and leaves our story, though not before leaving his testimony: "Life returns, life resumes and you cannot avoid its reality unless you cut your veins or hang yourself from a beam. I tried both, but in both cases there was always a hand, the hand of fate perhaps, to help me stop myself. When I was back home, after being in the extermination camp, and realized it would never be my home again because they were no longer in this world to share this same life with me—neither my children, my wife nor my close friends—when I realized I was alone, completely alone, I understood there were only two paths, death or life. And if I chose to live, though the wound would never heal, I'd have to press on, make money, earn my living day after day once again, shave every morning, laugh at what was funny, cry at what was sad. Except that sometimes I find the memory of Hurbinek intolerable, the child I saw die in Auschwitz, a very small child, sunk in a bunk, unable to overcome his permament shaking. I can never erase from my mind the sight of him dying; it always reminded me of the terrible pain and fear and helplessness my children must have felt in the hour of death."

5

Scholomo Buczko, the cobbler from Pomerania, opened a new cobblers in Bratislava, where he was taken in by cousins when he came back from Auschwitz. He married a teacher of Russian there and trade prospered. He only remembered Hurbinek four times in the whole of his life, the times, one could say, when he remembered The Camp (Buczko always said "The Camp" when he was referring to Auschwitz).

The first time was April 13, 1950. He left home and took a tram. There he read in a newspaper that they had put a price on the heads of 25,000 war criminals in Germany. For a few seconds he thought of Hurbinek's body in the abstract and thought that someone ought to pay for all that hurt they had inflicted.

The second time was June 21, 1953. When the game had just kicked off at a soccer field in his city, they opened the doors and placed a number of paralyzed and crippled children and adults behind the goals. From the terraces Buczko thought that if Hurbinek had lived he might have been one of those now leaning on crutches or using wheelchairs.

The third occasion was October 7, 1958. His wife gave birth to their fourth child and he held the baby for a few seconds in his arms. When he saw legs that were so weak and skin that was so white, he remembered the time he lifted Hurbinek up so Henek could change the blankets that were dirty with excrement for ones that were just as dirty. The concept of *clean* didn't exist in The Camp. The two children weighed the same, despite the age difference, and that was what brought to mind Hurbinek's tiny body.

The fourth was March 2, 1970, when Buczko was left paralyzed as the result of a car accident on the road to Prague. A drunken German (It just had to be a German! Buczko lamented to himself in later years) went through a traffic light and smashed smack into Buczko's Skoda. They took more than two hours to extract him from the twisted metal, but he didn't feel his legs in all that time. We know that he thought of Hurbinek for one last time. The prediction he'd always made that he would be linked to him for life was thus fulfilled.

6

Here is the eyewitness account of Yuri Chanicheverov, the nineteen-year-old Russian soldier who reached the Main Camp on the first day of March 1945 and looked through the window of the barrack where Hurbinek and the other sickly people were lodged.

"I had left the route the patrol was following. I couldn't deal with all those who were coming up to me and asking in Russian and Polish whether I'd come to execute or liberate them. They couldn't decide one way or the other when they saw I was armed. I stumbled over several bodies that were scattered here and there on the ashen ground. Some still flickered with life, breathed in short bursts, clinging to other inert bodies, skinny as starving dogs. That's when I wandered off and found myself opposite a window of a shack. Of all the horror we saw in that place, the unburied or half-buried corpses, the lunatics who walked by screaming hysterically, or the living dead who roamed as far as the barbed wire fences, and then threw themselves at them in order to keep standing, it was the inside of that shack crammed with sick people on rickety bunks that made the deepest impression on me. I could hear them moaning inside. They were frozen stiff, wrapped in blankets that stank as much as they did. The unpleasant smell hit me from the other side of the window. Immediately beneath the window I could see a child who filled no more than two or three palm-lengths of his bed. His face was tiny and sunken but his eyes bulged wide open. He was about to die at any second, or so it seemed, because he was surrounded by two other young people who were looking at him sorrowfully and holding his hands. He breathed anxiously, made a constant, hoarse noise, a forlorn moan, and kept shaking from pain that was beyond cure. His suffering was so awful in my eyes that I imagined how his little body that had almost ceased to exist contained all the horrors I had seen so far. I have never forgotten him and that day I think I learned once and for all the stark difference between pity and evil."

7

The nurse has switched off the light and gone. The room is now in shadows and perhaps it is time for a snooze, I'm not sure, but the nurse has given me a sedative. The fact is my legs were really hurting, the pain almost made me shout out. I miss Fanny and the children. I haven't alarmed them too much: it was quite a minor accident. I am really missing my life before I entered this hospital. But I tell myself to be patient and try to put my situation into perspective. They'll soon come to get me and I'll soon be home.

Nevertheless, I was going to Auschwitz, but not anymore.

I think about surviving, the very fact that I have passed by the gateway to death but not entered. Survival creates a degree of confusion, of bewilderment. Perhaps it is the greatest bewilderment a human being can ever face. If, for example, I think about Buczko, I get depressed. Like me, he had a car accident. Like him, I could have been left paralyzed. The sinister, curt Dr. Voghs had already said as much, "Broken knees, very bad, physiotherapy . . . but your spine is OK . . . fortunately." It would have been a very unjust irony of fate if I had traveled to Auschwitz to end up paralyzed like Hurbinek.

But I think about survival, about the harsh business of having to survive. For example, me. Now. Here.

Certainly, I am alive, but everything serves to remind me that I could be dead, that I *should* be dead: my car off to the scrapyard, my knees as well, smashed to smithereens, my face peppered with little cuts from the windshield glass, my clothes soaked in blood, my hands bandaged . . . The room is very similar to an autopsy room; the rest of the patients in this hospital, injured to a greater or lesser extent, have been operated on, are in pain, are confronting, to a greater or lesser extent, the fact that they have made it out of their trial with death well, that they have survived. Are re-making their lives.

Like those who survived Auschwitz. I dare say that and make the comparison. I have no right to, no right at all. I know that only too well, that it's insulting to compare my survival with theirs. But it is true that something, a unique reality, unites us: the fact that at some point in the chain of "life," neither they nor I raised the card that says "death," that's it. We are united by the death we left behind. Though, evidently, not all deaths are equal. Their horror was incalculable, arbitrary, devastating. Their horror is history's failure. Their horror cannot and must not be justified. Many live on afterward feeling guilty, wondering why they have survived, what makes them deserve life more than the others who died. A feeling of guilt that has led many to commit suicide. Others have re-made their lives, as best as they could, have created homes, had children, have tried to protect themselves from the pain of remembering. Others meet up periodically with their companions from the camps and keep alive the memory of the men, women and children who were murdered.

But I started this journey simply because I want Hurbinek to live a life he did not live, one that was snatched away. I want to give him that present, buy him years, birthday parties, if only that wasn't a delusion. I don't know what ghosts or lights or shadows inhabit the memories of survivors of Auschwitz. As far as I am concerned, I am only interested in the memory of Hurbinek they retain, the survival of Hurbinek in the future that opened up for some fortunate individuals when they crossed through the camp's barbed wire fences and returned to their past that had been destroyed. In how often and at what precise moments was Hurbinek remembered by those who knew, however briefly, of his equally brief existence. But I know that what I am attempting is impossible, and life has brought me to a halt here, in this Frankfurt hospital, so the frontier between my fictions and reality, in terms of Hurbinek, will continue to be blurred, porous and minimal.

8

We know that Berek Goldstein was fated to die in Auschwitz sooner or later and that was why he was recruited to work in a *Sonderkommando*. All those who worked in a *Sonderkommando* were sent to the gas chambers within a few months. Their execution was deferred, their suffering wasn't. They were forced to undress the people the SS selected every day to be exterminated with Zyklon B. They then entered the chambers and put the bluish bodies onto the trucks that transported them to the crematoria. First they had to cut off the girls and womens' hair and pull out the gold teeth, acts they sometimes carried out before executing them, depending on the volume of mass-produced dead to be processed. Many recognized their parents, wives and children among the victims. They put the bodies in the ovens and later emptied out their ashes. They had to crush any bones that had resisted.

Berek Goldstein had to undress his five-year-old son and leave him there amidst those screaming in the gas chamber, then take him to the oven and extract his ashes with a spade. He had to do so silently. He had to do so without crying or going crazy. He did consider the idea of throwing himself into the fire with his son's corpse in his arms. But was unable to do so because he was so befuddled by the whiplashes hitting him and the swift nature of the task. "*Schnell, Shnell, Schnell! Juda verrecke!*"[1] the German bawled until he was hoarse. But he did see how another companion in the *Sonderkommando*, a Jew from Dalmatia, did throw himself into the oven taking the SS standing next to him and aiming his automatic at him.

The dubious good fortune of Berek Goldstein resided in the fact that he was one of the last to carry out this horrible work and come out alive, even though diphtheria took him to the barrack where Hurbinek was. He never saw him, only heard him. He heard the whistle in his trachea, his weepy, wordless voice, that turned into a long piercing whine that suddenly stopped, as if all his exhausted energy had collapsed. From where he lay, Goldstein could barely see the blanket on the boy's bed go up and down to the rhythm of his gasps, and Henek coming and going

---

1   "Fast, fast, fast! Bear down, Jew!"

to his side with water or clothes. He wept a lot over him and his son.

We know that, when he was liberated, Berek Goldstein hung himself from a tree on the road to Katowice in April 1945. We know he hadn't lost his sanity and that it wasn't an attack of madness. On the contrary, he could still hear Hurbinek's moan, that melded in his mind with the image of his dead little son, naked in his arms, before he personally cast him into the flames.

9

Chaim Roth returned to Katowice only to stay a night in the station and hear the saddest news. He left Poland and established himself in Israel, first in Tel Aviv, and then, in 1958, in Jerusalem. In Tel Aviv he went into partnership with an old acquaintance from Katowice, Gus Lazar, who had also survived the Holocaust, and together they resumed their ice-cream business. Roth-Lazar ice-creams are still Israelis' favorite brand of ice-cream.

He didn't find any trace of the ghetto in Katowice. He discovered that all his family and friends had died, some executed by the *Einsatzkommandos* in the place of execution set up by the German-Romanian forces in the city outskirts, in the Yar Moriczim valley, between hills where blood ran like a stream, and the workers from his ice-cream factory died, alongside their wives and children. Others were murdered in the middle of the street, like his uncle Ravel and his cousin Yankel, killed by a bullet in the ear, the result of pure whim on the part of an SS officer, who said he saw them walking on the sidewalk when the anti-Jewish laws stipulated quite clearly that they could only walk on the road. Others had worse luck than Chaim in Auschwitz, like Ira his brother, who died in his arms totally out of his mind, in the bed next to Hurbinek's.

It must have been in 1973 when Chaim suddenly remembered Hurbinek. He was walking through the old city of Jerusalem, they were shooting a film and he stopped to watch the actors going through their routines. During a break, one thirstily drank water, because it was the hottest time of day. Chaim's mind returned to hell, as if he'd gone into a trance. He relived with a wealth of detail the time when he gave Hurbinek something to drink. That healthy young man, Henek, had given him a zinc can of water. The can was brimming over. He had filled it from a tin one of the Polish girls gave him, two nurses who avoided entering the barrack and did everything via young Henek, for whose love they competed. He supported the child's head, a head with only the sparsest clomps of hair, that fitted in the hollow of his hand. The boy was stiff and kept spasmodically moving his arms. A thread of air struggled to enter his nose. Chaim remembered how his neck seemed to dislocate and separate out from his head, and was very cold. Hurbinek's back was covered in sores and his open lips drooped. From Hurbinek's bed he looked at Ira his brother, who was dying and mad (he gnawned at his own fingers), but his brother smiled back at him despite his madness. When he came round, Chaim was pale and wan and leaning on the doorframe. He could hear the film crew shouting urgent instructions. He recovered and continued his walk until he was outside the city, summoning up more memories of that time, before his brother's delirious smile vanished.

10

We know that the Bohemian Franz Patzold was tortured and never forgot the face of his torturer, a Moldavian fascist they nicknamed Tod[2]. That led him to commit suicide one summer morning in 1981. We know that previously, under another name—François Fernández—he enrolled in the secret services of the French parachuters and infiltrated the Algerian FLN for several years. We know he was very introverted and shy and lived alone with a bird. His bad accent in any language protected him and helped him and his alibis. He never managed to become what he really wanted to be: a chef like his father living happily, in oblivion of everything and everybody. He could never throw off a feeling of humiliating rancor.

Throughout his life he often remembered Hurbinek, who had moved him deeply. If he had lived, he might have looked after him like a son. Patzold was one of those, along with Henek and Primo Levi, who most tried to understand one of the words that child had uttered, since they presumed he was speaking Bohemian, given that there was some similarity between his name, if it was such, and the word for "meat" in the Bohemian language. Patzold took it in turns with Henek to put his ear close to the child's lips and try to understand what

---

2   Death, in German.

he was muttering amid his hoarse, panting breath. He used to caress and kiss him. When Patzold committed suicide, he looked back in time and found few moments of tenderness in his life. Hurbinek involved one, perhaps the only one. The rest of his life was filled with hatred, because he never found Tod the Moldavian who tortured him with shears.

11

There were others who found out about Hurbinek's existence and shared the air with him in that improvised infirmary shack, but they never remembered him afterward.

That was the case of Jan Vesely, a Hungarian. He joined the Communist Party and devoted himself to municipal politics, and became notorious for his ability to give speeches. A housing estate on the outskirts of Budapest was named after him until 1988.

And that was also the case of the Slovak Ahmed Yildirim, who opened a pet shop in Sarajevo and cared for many sick baby animals, to such an extent that he became a renowned specialist. He was shot dead by a Serbian sniper in 1994.

And the case of Manuel Valiño who returned to Madrid after spending a long time in refugee camps throughout Europe, and from there left for Buenos Aires and under the pseudonym of Alfredo Martel became famous in Hollywood where his traces are lost and he departs our story like a ghost.

And the case of David Bogdanowski, a Polish Jew from Warsaw, who was traumatized at the roll call in Auschwitz-Birkenau when they slit open his father's belly in front of everyone and filled his guts with iron shavings and empty cartridges, then threw powder on them and set them on fire, simply because he was deaf and didn't reply when they called out his name. Bogdanowski married an ambulance driver in Israel where he still lives. We know that he roamed the streets of Warsaw in those first days of the liberation trying to find some clue as to the origins of Hurbinek, but soon realized he had found no reliable data and dropped it.

And the case of the Frenchmen, Joseph Grosselin and Auguste Friedel. Both went back to Paris and became friends. They worked in banking, and prospered separately in different entities. They met now and then in the synagogue, generally once a year, and then ate in L'Agricole, a Paris restaurant where they talked and recalled the desperate days of extermination, trying to ensure nobody was missed by their memories or in their prayers. But Hurbinek was never present. They forgot him, as they forgot many others who, in all their good will, they didn't even realize they were forgetting.

12

The hospital room has got much lighter. Who are these people here with me? One, says the nurse, died yesterday and I didn't even know who it was. He was in the bed opposite but is no longer there. Was he young or old, did he die of cancer, or because of an accident, during an operation, or was he shot or stabbed, does he leave children, did he love, work, did he like aeroplanes? I know nothing about him. Or about the others. What can they possibly know about me?

Share. Bump into. See each other again. These are verbs only time makes possible. If Hurbinek had lived, he might have bumped into Ernst Sterman in an American spa for those suffering from chronic tuberculosis, or he might have said hello to Scholomo Buczko at the end of a soccer game he'd got into free because he was paralyzed, or he might have become a partner in Chaim Roth's ice-cream business and now the most famous ice-creams in Israel might carry his name, or he might have helped Franz Patzold, now declared his adoptive father, to find the Moldavian who tortured him, or, on a trip to Moscow, he might have bumped into Yuri Chanicheverov, now a taxi driver or museum guide, who would be curious about the sight of that man with crutches, or shared a table in L'Agricole with Joseph Grosselin and Auguste Friedel the bankers though not one of those three recognized him, or drunk coffee with his friend Primo Levi on an avenue in Turin and both would silently remember Berek Goldstein and Rubem Yetzev, or wept with Claricia Novaceanu at the burial of Henek, the hero, on a cold day in Hungary, in 1956.

And yet Hurbinek did live on in these lives, in some way.

VI

THAT GAP THERE IN THE COLLARBONE

1

It is impossible not to think about the children the Nazis killed or about the cruel, savage means they employed. And it's impossible for anyone who knows not to writhe at the thought. When thinking about Hurbinek, when creating Hurbinek's universe, it is equally impossible to leave aside the thousands, hundreds of thousands of Jewish and non-Jewish children, like him, who were crushed by that criminal German whirlwind.

Killing a child is easy, killing thousands of children is even easier, but it isn't at all easy to erase the memory of children after they are massacred. I'm not sure why, I sometimes think it is because the lives of dead children are lives that were not lived and that must exist as fables, in a kind of timeless limbo set in history, their unredeemed presence returning to wreak a just revenge. If I believed in ghosts, I would only believe in the ghosts of massacred children.

But prostrated in this hospital bed my eyes suddenly meet those of a youngish child, I guess he must be six—double Hurbinek's age when he died. He is sitting in one of the hospital chairs next to a bed at the end of our small ward. He looks at me now and then, quizzically. He is licking an ice-cream. He has come with a young woman I imagine to be his mother. I can see a man with a thick beard in that far bed, perhaps his father or uncle, or even his elder brother. His head is bandaged. They are all very young and dark-skinned.

I look away from that child and look up to see yet again that slice of blue sky through the barred window. That child made my mind fly off to Vienna and an extraordinary woman, Erika Fisherkant. When Fanny and I met her in 1991, she was still living in Cologne and the Foundation that bears her name was just getting off to a start. Her house was above an inn, in a side street very close to the re-built Gothic cathedral, and the place was packed with half-opened boxes, tall filing cabinets and colored folders that were scrupulously organized and labeled containing all kinds of documentation. It seemed highly chaotic simply because so much was crammed in and because people were continuously rushing in and out. It happened, very inopportunely, to be the day when they were moving for the nth time to a larger building. Three other women worked with her, whose names I never got to know, and a very Polish man whom Erika introduced to us as Tadeusz, her fiancé. Fanny and I helped them move and we became great friends that day.

The Erika Fisherkant Foundation devotes itself, or devoted itself up to a month ago, to the investigation of the crimes the Nazis committed against children. A month ago I heard that Erika Fisherkant had been recently murdered in her office. A man walked in and shot her point blank in the head. He has yet to be arrested as I was well reminded by a copy of the *Frankfurter Allgemeine Zeitung* that I'd been reading in the hospital over the last few days.

Her Foundation's headquarters had been based in Vienna for two years, in the Ringen. She didn't like Haider's Vienna but recognized it was now symbolically important to be there. And that was the last I heard from Erika, when she wrote and told me she wasn't sure whether to go to Tel Aviv or settle down in Austria. She chose Europe and stayed in Vienna, although ever since she had received death threats and threats of other abuse from neo-Nazis and rightwing extremists. In the letter to me in which she expressed her doubts she wrote, "I am German, I can't do what I do here in Israel, I would lose all credibility. And here, with a bit of luck, I will end up earning the martyr's reputation that is just what my guilty conscience as a German woman requires."

Erika was a tiny, brave woman, between fifty-eight and sixty, originally from Dresden, who had worked as a critical, incisive historian in various German universities, focusing her research on the massacres of Jews from the East perpetrated by the Nazis between 1941 and 1944. The fate of the weakest, of the children, soon made a deep impact on her. Something was unlocked within her, and changed the course of her life, when she heard eyewitness accounts of the horrible death in Auschwitz of a four-year-old boy, Ansel Bloch.

It happened like this. One April morning in 1943, Ansel was forced to kneel and make the sign of the cross with his arms. When his arms were exhausted and dropped down, an SS officer went over and stuck a knife in his legs, but didn't kill him. They forced him to kneel down again, his arms in a cross, while he bled in sight of everyone. The child cried and his arms dropped down again, three or four times. The officer finally approached him with a man in a white coat, perhaps one of the camp doctors; both were smiling. The officer was carrying his knife: the man in the white coat pointed to a very precise spot on Ansel's body and said, "That gap there in the collarbone."

The officer drove his knife in between that soft, white bone and blood spurted out. Four-year-old Ansel fell down dead. His parents were forced to observe him being tortured, because they wouldn't allow them to faint. Ansel's father survived and related those cruel events to Erika. His voice, she recalls, resonated with a deep, solemn, respectful sadness, as if he were reading a passage from the Bible.

2

Erika Fisherkant unearthed reports, whether by the Nazis themselves or Soviet investigators, and assembled an impressive array of eyewitness accounts and gradually became absolutely committed to preserving the memories of all those children who died so brutally and so arbitrarily.

"Arbitrarily?" she would correct me. "Nothing was arbitrary. There wasn't the degree of arbitrariness you might conclude from the official version that depicts only a handful of murdering Nazis were to blame for everything and the rest simply carried out orders, as if all the other millions of Germans who embraced the anti-Jewish laws and were aware, to a lesser or greater degree, of the final decision to exterminate the whole Jewish people, belonged to a civilian army that implemented orders imposed by the Nazi Party. Orders? Under what threat? Was each German citizen, man, woman or child perhaps forced to kill a couple of Jews to earn the right to be a good, upstanding German? They weren't forced to, but I know a huge majority did so, to a certain extent, simply by looking the other way. I am a German woman and have always been quite suspicious of that version that removed blame. As many others are, and, naturally, I am not and will never be the only one. My father died in Stalingrad and in his final letters, with censored sentences and his crossings out, between the lines he said we were all mad and that history would judge us mercilessly for what we were doing. It was a brief illumination on his part, because my father was no innocent man, I'm sure he had a lot of blood on his hands, he was a an out-and-out SS, a member of their police batallions. My father killed children, I'm almost sure he did."

Erika Fisherkant said that in 1991 and her work has fulfilled her spirit of atonement. She created her Foundation so nobody would forget the children. Who could have murdered her? Did some neo-Nazi hothead carry out his threat? Was a Foundation like hers still uncomfortable for a country like Austria that has a lot left to purge? They are still investigating her case.

Back to the children, Erika's obsession. Killing children is easy. But it was even easier for an SS, since it was like killing a small insect, and for an SS a Jewish child was a small insect or even less, since it lacked any human spirit, which meant it was legitimate to eliminate them and they could do so with total impunity.

Children, especially if they are very young, leave barely a trace. They don't write letters, leave written or oral accounts in their wake, don't draw up documents, contracts, receipts, don't own valuable objects, aren't remembered by their community because of any common gesture or action, have few friends, and the ones they do have are other children. They live cheek-by-jowel with their families, their parents, their brothers and sisters, the photos in which they appear are family photos, where it is almost impossible to identify even the adults. And if the adults disappear with them, no one, ever, will call them to mind in even the most fleeting of reflections.

For Erika Fisherkant those children that no one remembers because no one is alive to remember them deserve special commemoration, in active protest against the grotesque, complacent unravelling of history. Her project was to find the tiniest details and trace the names and surnames, origins, families, towns, streets and the past geography of the largest possible number of children murdered by the Nazis. The vast majority of those children were Jewish.

Erika Fisherkant knew—of course she knew, because she was there and survived!—that on February 13, 1945, a few days before Hurbinek died, the RAF bombed

Dresden and laid the city waste. Thousands of German civilians died, including some of Erika's cousins and friends. But she used to reply to her detractors who said she was biaised: "I know that many children died, but none like Ansel Bloch, for example. Perhaps all deaths are the same, but they aren't equal. There are differences. The only one who was guilty was Hitler. In a way, he killed all those children, the ones belonging to others and ours; he poisoned us all."

3

Erika Fisherkant took a long time to get the children's weeping out of her dreams. Sometimes, she would relate, she woke up *aware* she had been dreaming of fear pure and simple, without faces, situations or concrete acts you might call nightmares: she dreamed of fear in a pure form, as if it were a universal category that made her tremble at night in bed. She didn't dream of her experience of fear, but the accumulated experience of fear of all those children before they died. She came to suffer a kind of chronic, self-inflicted insomnia out of fear that she might dream that fear once again.

Erika's research was horrific. "They are facts I know and that I cannot pretend I don't know," she would say.

I remember how she once let me see the cards where she had noted down eyewitness accounts or events related to her searches. It was my own private walk through human terror, and that was how I discovered the gap in the collarbone could assume many different forms.

Like Erika Fisherkant, I discovered that in a village in Byelorussia they selected a woman and her two children, aged five and seven, from the line. Without saying a word, they cut the head off one in front of the mother and shot the other in the face. They let her live on for a day so her suffering didn't end quickly. Then they killed her.

I discovered that in Babi Yar the children fell either alive or severely wounded into the graves where they carried out mass executions. They fell on top of their dead mothers and wept for a long time until they were finally suffocated by the next round of corpses that buried them.

I discovered that they systematically smashed the heads of one or two-year-old babies against the road in the outskirts of ghettos.

I discovered that they cut off the breasts of twelve to fourteen-year-old girls in public before executing them.

I discovered that a huge SS on the platform in Auschwitz picked up a child by his hair with one hand and shot him in the ear with the other.

I discovered that in a village in Ukraine the police batallions crushed boys' testicles under their boots before shooting them.

I discovered that sometimes, to amuse themselves, German soldiers would lift up a child by both ears and shake it several times in the air until its ears were ripped off its body. They laughed and nailed the ears to wooden posts.

I discovered that the Germans always laughed at their own brutality toward children. It was significant or atrocious for them. It was like destroying nests of sparrows or pigeons with their eggs. In these cases, they were only little Jewish chicks. Others needed to drink before they could kill children.

I discovered that in Crematorium 5 in Auschwitz the SS threw live children into the ovens.

I discovered that in a village in Lithuania several soldiers approached a group of children with their mothers. As soon as they were alongside them, on the spur of the moment, they suddenly took out their swords and knives and started to skewer the children. Not one managed even a whimper. It was such a shock. Their mothers went crazy before they died.

4

When it's time for my daughters' birthdays, I feel in a wild party mood. Fanny often tells me I become just one more child, a child like them and that the week before I'm all excited thinking the day is round the corner and that it will be spectacular. Come what may, the whole day is devoted to them, it's a party for every member of the family, no one works, no one does anything routine, everything is special: the food is more lavish, the day's timetable more uncharted (unlimited freedom to schedule things as the whim takes us), the clothes we wear are more random, the words we exchange less inhibited and every unexpected detail prompts jokes and laughter. I am an optimist, as Fanny says. The day before I buy presents for everyone, including Fanny and myself. And my own private ritual: our home dawns full of phigonias, Fanny's favorite yellow flowers. That is how I want to celebrate that my daughters were born, and are alive and will live for a long time to come. My daughters' birthdays—Mina in January and Zoe in June—are really gifts to me, and I cherish them mentally in my memory, scrupulously, as Fanny cherishes the memory of the phigonias I gave her. I treasure every year that passes with them and treasure the days that remind me how my life and theirs have experienced another year and become part of a common history that makes us what we are—together and alive—I don't ever want to forget this, trivialize or take it for granted, because it is a gift amid all the suffering that has existed or will exist in the world—and I'd pay whatever price was necessary to guarantee that every birthday takes place inexorably, until, when they are older, they can decide by themselves how they'd like to celebrate their birthdays. Today I would buy lots of birthdays for Hurbinek. Today I would buy lots of birthdays for the children whose deaths are described on Erika Fisherkant's record cards.

5

Shove, knock down, terrorize, beat, disembowel, spit on, open up, slash, insult, tear apart, aim at, shoot, execute, nail down, throw down, dismember, hang, crush, decapitate, inject, trepan, disfigure, amputate, triturate, burn, strike, stab, electrocute, rape, infect, torture, deceive, drill, inflate, behead, cut, skewer, bury, strangle, beat and tear apart are verbs the Nazis applied to children.

I don't know how much blood from children in Auschwitz and other camps was used for transfusions for the wounded of Stalingrad and other eastern fronts, but it was a lot. The biggest real act of vampirism in the whole of history. Erika's Foundation opened a line of investigation into the use of children who were forced to be "providers" of blood and skin for people with burns. The dossiers were labelled TRANSFUSIONS or GRAFTS. The doctors in Auschwitz began to siphon blood from many children and adolescents, when there began to be a general shortage in Germany from 1942. It was considered wasteful to send them to the gas chambers without making use of their blood and their skin that was used in grafts needed by soldiers who'd suffered serious burns, whose faces, arms and legs needed reconstructing for aesthetic reasons. Didn't the Reich make use of the clothes, hair and teeth of the undesirables it was gassing? Well, why not get blood from children, from the healthiest—they won't be needing it! It was clearly reasoning based on a sound grasp of logic and economics.

In 1943 many of these children were moved to field hospitals, where they were shot dead as soon as they'd done with them, then buried in trenches that had been abandoned or blown open by mortar fire. For many years people believed that those children had died according to the usual Auschwitz procedures.

The idea was Josef Mengele's, better known in the camp as the Angel of Death, and it came to him as a result of a vision inspired by a crucifix his mother Walburga had given him. Walburga Mengele was extremely religious and brought her three children up to be strictly observant Roman Catholics on the farm where they were born in Günzburg in central Bavaria. She gave each of them a mother-of-pearl crucifix that Josef always carried with him, that had been blessed by the Bishop of Ulm, the nearby regional capital and a city that Ahasver, the wandering Jew, once visited, something the Mengele family probably didn't know. The blood running down Christ's body on the cross gave him the idea when he was a lieutenant on the Ukraine front in 1941. He traveled across the Ukraine as commanding officer of a terrible *SS Einsatzkommando*. It isn't difficult to imagine his batallion cleaning out villages and surrendering to the orgies of extermination that film-maker Elem Klimov recreates so admirably, so starkly in his films. His ideas about using the blood of children and adolescents were immediately backed by Himmler and Eichmann, who used to receive his absurd reports on the unheard-of genetic possibilities opened up by his experiments in the terrain of human inheritance. He started to put them into practice in 1943 when he reached Auschwitz as a doctor to carry out his experimentation on the impurity of inferior, non-Aryan races.

His name still makes my hair stand on end and even more so when I see photos of him as an old man in Paraguay in the 1970s. Ever since I began to watch documentaries on the Second World War, one name has always terrified me: Mengele. There is something primitive about the three euphonious syllables of his name, as if he were a kind of monstruous, if not unreal, wizard. And yet, just like Adolf

Eichmann, he was a man who looked ordinary and was cold and calculating in a methodical, mean way.

Even more primitive for me in this German hospital, where I feel at the mercy of doctors I don't trust, who I know I'm ludicrously satanizing, like the dreadful Voghs (he's probably a good guy, I'm sure he is), doctors with a priestly streak like Mengele, capable of experimenting on me, coldly and cruelly, like Mengele, who thought that his human guinea pigs were degraded, worthless beings. And consequently I am really distressed to be in Frankfurt, marooned like a ship without sails, in that city where Mengele studied and graduated in Medicine in the summer of 1938, the year when he enlisted in the evil *Schutzstaffel*, more lethally known as the SS. He was 28 and aspired to broaden the scope of German science.

7

Josef Mengele was barely a doctor aspiring to a future in the Third Reich when he met the man who was to be his protector and patron, Professor Otmar von Verschuer, director of the Kaiser William Berlin Institute for Anthropology and an influential member of the National-Socialist Party. Von Verschuer opened the doors to the fantasies of genetic experimentation: Hitler's slogan about purifying the race needed a solid, indisputable, and above all, scientific base, and the young doctor decided to devote himself tirelessly to that end. He had been summoned to *create* a whole new race, the thousand-year race, and that was much more sublime and less tawdry than purifying it.

Thanks to his military merits—he was decorated with the First Class Iron Cross for his *cleansing actions* in the Ukraine—Mengele ensured that Auschwitz was given over to him as one huge laboratory where he would have complete freedom to carry out his experiments. And he took his responsibility seriously as a scientist who must carry out genuine *field work* and descended into that infected pool of filth, that sewer of Jews, where it was unpleasant though necessary to work, although, as he recognized, it was also an extremely exciting challenge for a man of science. It was the price to pay for the universal prestige he was sure would be his.

He was brutal.

He experimented on some 3,000 children, mainly Jews and gypsies, of which barely 200 survived in a chronically sick or deformed state. On the basis of a cursory glance as soon as the trains reached Auschwitz, the tireless Mengele made his own selection of the children he deemed suitable for his research, and put to his left or his right those he chose for the infirmary barrack in Camp B or to send straight to the gas chambers.

Mengele's great speciality was physical pain. More specifically, his experiments focused on physical pain as suffered by children. He wanted to know everything on the subject and experimented collaterally with thresholds of pain, inasmuch as he practised on twins in order to try out perverted, unlikely techniques of genetic engineering. To that end he carried out arbitrary castrations of twin girls without anaesthetics, and thus achieved two experiments in one: he studied their genitals, almost always without proper technical means or medical preparation, in order to analyze manifestations of pain, such as screams, contractions, exudations, despair, fainting, shaking and stiffness, among others.

One can conceive of no greater cruelty or sadism than the dissections that he, with the help of other camp doctors, carried out on children who died suffering the greatest pain. Or lunatic experiments in which he injected two or three-year-old children with huge quantities of petrol or phenol to ascertain how long and in what state blood clots in the human body under the impact of synthetic, embalming liquids. Or stomach operations carried out without anesthetics, simply to study why entrails occupy such and such a place in the body and not some other.

Mengele didn't perform by himself. He undertook and completed his experiments with the connivance, praise and real assistance he received from the doctors and nurses of Auschwitz, some of whom were proud to be invited by Mengele to associate their names with the advances for the future of science, like Koenig, who was interested in experimenting sadistically on dwarves. But that future was neither grandiose nor glorious. Mengele had to flee from Auschwitz on January 17, 1945 and hide on his farm in Günzburg as an ordinary laborer. He then entered a monastery where he stayed under a false identity until 1949 when he made it to Argentina without too much difficulty. His death, whenever it happened, came as insufficient pay for the horror he left behind him. There is, or was, in the Erika Fisherkant Foundation a huge archive of hundreds of cases that are still open and it was labeled: JOSEF MENGELE, TORMENTOR.

I discovered that in a village in eastern Poland, Piasky put naked children in cages that he then buried while they were still alive.

I discovered that a child was thrown from a truck onto a street in Lublin by his mother so he could escape. A German soldier picked him up by the leg and threw him violently against the wheels of another oncoming truck. The child died, run over in full view of his mother.

I discovered they split open many children's heads against rocks and tree trunks. It was common practice and saved on ammunition and unnecessary effort.

I discovered that in some towns in the Ukraine the *Waffen SS*—to which Mengele belonged—would organize a big spectacle by building a big bonfire into the flames of which they threw live children in front of their parents. A child ran out of one of these bonfires, screaming horribly, hair and hands on fire. They forced him back into the fire with a pitchfork.

I discovered that many children from Gorlice, in Galicia, had their heads smashed by blows from rifle butts, while those doing it tried to outdo one another seeing who could shout the loudest, in a soldierly sporting competition. They did it with such might that brains flew everywhere.

I discovered they beat children with their fists until they lost consciousness.

I discovered that they let some parents in Krakow choose between strangling their children themselves or allowing them to be skewered on bayonets. Most felt compelled to kill their children with their own hands.

I discovered that they made children in Treblinka walk in columns for hours until they were exhausted. They shot in the head any who dropped behind from exhaustion.

I discovered that in towns in Russia and Byelorussia, in the places they chose to carry out mass executions, they broke the children's spines by beating them with wooden stakes. They took several hours to die.

I discovered that German mothers dressed their children in clothing that came from the dead bodies of Jewish children.

9

I wonder what state Hurbinek's collarbone must have been in and how long Dr. Mengele examined it before he discarded him, that January morning when an SS medical officer, a *Lagerarzt*, walked into the Ka-Be—the initials used to refer to the camp infirmaries, that were called *Krankenbau*—with the two-and-a-half, perhaps even three-year-old baby, perhaps even on his birthday, the last birthday he would ever have. He must have found him in a double wall in one of the barracks or perhaps someone handed him over in exchange for a last-minute favor. Rather than kill him, the *Lagerarzt* thought of Mengele's scientific work.

Perhaps it happened like that or perhaps it didn't. At any rate, neither Primo Levi, nor Henek, nor Franz Patzold, nor anyone else, could ever have known since the prisoners didn't know about Mengele's experiments. But the number tattooed on his small arm could be explained by that visit to Mengele's infirmary. That number on the arm of a three-year-old child was proof that he had passed through one of the *Selektzie*, selections made by the Angel of Death. Consequently, the answer to the question Levi asks about the pain Hurbinek suffered before reaching the barrack that brought them all together might be that the child was kept alive, like a guinea pig, in Mengele's cages.

The injection of a small dose of petrol, depending where it is made, can lead to permanent paralysis, because the whole area of body affected is rendered useless. To ensure the remaining blood doesn't clot, a rapid puncture or deep cut must be implemented in the section above the injected area, to prevent septicemia. When Mengele observed Hurbinek's collarbone and that white gap, almost a membrane next to the skinny neck, he considered possibly injecting carbolic acid. He was sure the immediate clotting of the blood in the brain would trigger a muscular spasm throughout the body. He'd read in a book about neurology that was what happened to rats. Perhaps it also happened to men as well, and perhaps even to children?

However, he had a change of mind. Thus, Hurbinek's paralysis wouldn't derive from a limited injection of petrol, as it had gelled in Mengele's mind for a few minutes. Hurbinek's paralized legs, the uselessness of his organs from the waist down, would derive from one of Mengele's stupid experiments that consisted in separating out vertebrae by inserting a wedge made of the bone from another child's vertebra in the spine, the purpose being to see what would be the level of acceptance and what side effects might be produced by the contact between the two different bones. These most peculiar experiments on the backbone formed part of Mengele's favorite operations. He believed—absurdly—that the key to purifying races resided in the backbone.

A few minutes after Mengele's savage surgical operation, little Hurbinek was strapped on a bunk and placed under observation without food. His screams died down and gave way to the terror that silenced him and made him shake. They left him there to die; Mengele refused to waste bullets.

10

I discovered that when they were destroying the ghettos in cities, on a whim, they lifted children up by the neck and threw them violently down from windows and balconies of high flats, or down stairwells.

I discovered that sometimes, when the SS were in a hurry, they strangled children where they found them.

I discovered that in the city of Grodno, the Germans helped the children to strip, then shot them in the back of the neck, one by one.

I discovered that they snatched babies from their mothers' arms, grabbing them by a leg, and threw them violently into the lorries, thus breaking their necks.

I discovered that two or three SS would violently pull apart one-year-old babies.

I discovered that in the Chelmno camp they would hang children in front of their parents.

I discovered that in the village of Svisloc they threw the babies up in the air so that others, in the spirit of a clay pigeon shoot, could fire at them while they hurtled through the air. They then fell into the ditches where they had placed their wounded mothers to be buried once they had watched that macabre game of target practice.

11

Parents, whenever they could, said goodbye to their children, knowing that in a few hours they would never be together again, that they would shortly die, and die painfully. Today I wonder what that moment would be like, the goodbye to my children, if they gave me that opportunity, after informing me that they would be murdered, shot, beheaded or gassed in a few hours. I am incapable of conceiving such a farewell; it is impossible, I cannot conceive such a final farewell. Let alone imagine it.

VII

ACTORS IN A MINIATURE THEATER

1

The life of Pavel Farin

I felt under a responsibility to give Hurbinek a future and that occasionally led me to look for him concealed within the personality of a man called Pavel Farin. Or rather to believe—as Fanny later said—that if Hurbinek had lived on, he might be that Pavel Farin who appeared as such a happy find. Perhaps Hurbinek really lives on as that individual, Farin the Russian. A life that was inserted, decided by me, the creator of his future. Why not? Why couldn't he have more lives? Other possible lives?

I came across him when he was some fifty-three years old. Fanny and I had gone to the theater, one autumnal night in 1995, to see a performance by a contemporary dance company named after its director and lead dancer, Claude Schlumberger. Our attention was riveted in every act by the dramatic, baroque, bubbly, explosively colorful stage sets. I searched the programme for the name of the set designer and costume designer. And yes, there it was: Pavel Farin, a name that at the time meant absolutely nothing to me, but was renowned in the world of dance. The performance was extremely polished and the final applause from the audience was never-ending. All the dancers came out and bowed, as did Schlumberger himself, sweating and clutching a bouquet of flowers, alongside a man on crutches who had a dreadful limp. He stood at one end of the stage. A spotlight focused on him. The director introduced him as Pavel Farin, the great costume designer. I then saw that he was supporting his whole body with the crutches and practically dragged his legs behind him. Why couldn't he be Hurbinek?

When the Red Army arrived and liberated the camp in Auschwitz, Hurbinek survived. Quite miraculously, it must be said, since some of his key organs had begun to fail as a result of Mengele's lunacy, and his paralysis hinted at the future decay of his lower limbs. On February 27, 1945 he was transferred by Russian nurses who took pity on that human remnant that was half child, half nothing. First they put him in an ambulance crammed with wounded and then in a hospital train that went to Moscow, where he became one of hundreds of thousands of orphaned children who were distributed between state bodies throughout the Soviet Union. In Hurbinek's case, given his physical condition and moribund state of health, it was decided not to send him to a far-flung province, where he would be certain to die because he was so weak due to a lack of medical resources. Doctors in Moscow's Central Hospital took him on and gave him a thorough examination, and he was considered to be a special case and was sent here and there, and in a few years, quite remarkably, he recovered part of his bodily functions, even his speech. But it was a long time before he was able to walk, after numerous operations that restored some feeling, though very little, to the lower part of his torso. The aftermath of those many operations on his hips and spine to find out why he was so immobile would be that he would always have to drag his feet and rely on crutches, as Fanny and I saw on that stage set in Madrid. It is most likely that Hurbinek would have lived with other children at the expense of the state in the Communist Colony no. 1 for Victims of the Patriotic War, based at 7 Ulitsa Engelskaya, which he would only leave when he had appointments for treatment on the Central Hospital at Kalinin Prospekt. He was brought up in the Colony, in the section for orphans, by Party bureaucrats who explained why that strange number was tattooed on his arm—those numbers that never faded however hard he rubbed—but they never told him he was Jewish, or that maybe his parents were, because they never mentioned his parents, and, indeed, what sense would it have made to do that, if they were only ashes, ashes that were unfortunately not simply ashes. They merely saw him as one more Russian child, abandoned and anonymous in a death camp, victim of the aggressive turn taken by History. Hurbinek, the name they gave him in that Auschwitz infirmary, in his most recent, but very distant past, was a word he found inscrutable, immediately rejected and literally erased from his mind. He would never utter the word again. They then gave him the name of Pavel Farin because one of those bureaucrats did supply him with a first name and surname (though nothing else; Hurbinek never saw him again), a mere administrative means of registering orphans found in the camps as legitimate citizens and avoiding difficulties for their adoptive families, since there wasn't really an adoption process, only red tape so the state could look after them. The majority, especially the older children, were then conscripted into the Red Army. Now definitively converted into Pavel Farin, Hurbinek learned Russian, that he always considered to be his mother tongue, and it would be several years before he suspected his real origins. He had been saved. (Or rather, I rescued him.)

At the age of thirteen Pavel started to walk with the support of crutches, in 1955, when he started his apprenticeship in a theater scenery workshop, the Igor Landau Workshop for the Decorative Arts, at 26 Ulitsa Serafimovich in Moscow. He was immediately attracted by the half solemn, half ironic colors of the illuminated manuscripts and medieval paintings, in the great variety of reproductions held in Landau's collections. They used them to inspire the craftsmen in the workshops who were making backcloths and costumes for the classical works performed on stage and in the cinema with popular actors like Cherkasov or Boliyedev or dancers at the Bolshoi, stars like Ermoleyev and Plisetskaya. By the age of twenty, Pavel had already drawn and painted at the Landau all the sets for the operas that he came to love over time: *Boris Godunov*, *The Marriage of Figaro*, *Rigoletto*, *Il Trovatore*, and *Carmen*; or for famous ballets like Khrennikov's *Love for Love* and Pushkin's *Mozart and Salieri*, or for plays in vogue: Gorky's *Summerfolk*, Alexei Tolstoy's *Tsar Fyodor*, Chekov's *The Seagull*, and hundreds of other works. New worlds, full of playfulness and whimsy, that he could create as he wished, and even create as works unique on the face of the world. For the first time in his life he felt happy. He learned the trade of poster art and studied Russian iconography from the twenties and thirties. He imitated his favorite, Gustav Klucis. He became expert and was much in demand in Moscow's theaterland. He grew up drawing and painting nonstop. At twenty-five, he took a position at the prestigious Comedy and Drama Theater on Ulitsa Jalova, directed by Liubimov. This was a very famous theater popular with Moscovites, who began to call it by the name of the nearest subway station: the Taganskaya. Pavel began as third dressing room assistant and was not granted permission to travel with the company. He became familiar with the repertory that was sometimes considered too liberal for the mood of the times in the USSR: Mayakovsky, Pushkin, Brecht, Bulgakov and Sholokhov. Helped by his cruel physique, by the end of the year Pavel was using his dark sense of humor and acerbic critical spirit to shape his artistic personality. Many felt he liked to pose as a *maudit*, or was blinded by bitterness, though others considered him to be an artist blinded by the gods. He devoured the Russian classics. The Taganskaya gradually incorporated into its repertory as their own many of Pavel Farin's creations, and by 1970 he was the company's premier set-designer, had four assistants and all the iconography the theater produced was his: costumes, posters, curtains, stage sets, brochures, and make up. Liubimov drew up the season's programme with him, and his opinions were very present both in the official and clandestine press. The sight of that frail man standing only with the support of his crutches made him appear extremely fragile and soon became familiar in all theaters, and he became a prestigious, even mythical figure. People felt a mixture of pity and admiration for the backcloths, stage sets and costumes created by a man who was so deformed in the lower part of his body, with legs floating like loose sticks in trouser legs that seemed to contain nothing at all. Almost pathetically thin, grasping a sempiternal glass of vodka, Pavel, who spurned the sun, possessed a pallid, phantom aspect that well suited the persona of a saturnine artist. Inevitably, as if predestined, though he was completely unaware of the process, old traces began to appear on his face of Hurbinek, that strange child he once was and would never recognize.

2

The life of Jozsef Kolunga

Or else Hurbinek metamorphosed into an employee of the Budapest Tram System, one Jozsef Kolunga, who was promoted at twenty-eight to the rank of inspector for repairs at the terminal in Zsigmont Móricz Square, where line 61 started. His promotion had been hotly contested, his rivals being two companions considered to be "healthy" and who, unlike Jozsef, didn't move around on bothersome crutches. However, a lot was owed to the influence of Ferenc Kolunga, his adoptive father, a tram driver who entered the System in the thirties and ended up being a legend, a point of reference for workers since he personified both class and patriotic pride. Many brave feats of his were recounted, the greatest of which was perhaps when he saved 230 Jewish children in 1944, at the end of the war, when the Nazis began to transport hundreds of thousands of Hungarian Jews to Auschwitz, where they were thrown into the crematoria upon arrival, with no intermediate stages at all. Ferenc Kolunga risked his life when he moved those children across the city, crouching on the floor of his tram as they passed through German checkpoints, until he could hide them in one of the terminals, perhaps the very same terminal where on his birthday in 1970 his son is now celebrating his promotion. He isn't his son exactly, or is, depending on how you look at it. What happened was that, at the end of the war someone in the Soviet Red Cross told him about a tiny three-year-old boy, who couldn't walk, and who had appeared in an infirmary in the Polish camp in Auschwitz. Nobody knew where he came from; maybe he was Hungarian or Bohemian. The memory of how he had saved those children only a year ago was still fresh in his mind, and he took the boy, whom he brought up as his own son, although he was a bachelor. Father and son always lived alone like that: Ferenc cared for Jozsef, Ferenc's inevitable heir. The legs of little Jozsef (since he was baptized with that name as a Catholic in the Central Parish Church) strengthened and when he could walk, his father started to take him to the Tram System's canteen, and later on to the workshops, and even later, to the offices where he sat an examination and started working in the supplies department. He dealt with paperwork, administration and spent his days filling in forms to apply for spare parts. Every day on his walk to work from the family house in Belváros Jozsef would cross the Szabadság bridge early, stop opposite Béla Bartók Avenue (whose music he adored, especially his string quartets, practically the official music of the Kolunga household) and watch the trams pass by, with their chrome-plating, sluggish speed and the bewitching mechanical hum of their condensors. He sometimes jumped on one and, as he was wearing his uniform, the drivers let him share the driver's seat. He knew he could never drive one of those beautiful vehicles, but he came that close, very close to doing so. Traveling there was most like what he longed to do—to drive a tram. He often jumped aboard an empty tram in the terminal, when it was standing empty in its shed, and sat behind the handle, dreaming he was driving across the city, as his father had so often done. Ferenc was the leader of the Budapest tram drivers, and that made his son very proud. From his office desk, Jozsef could also see that the post of workshop inspector, essential for keeping a check on the departures and arrivals of trams, was not beyond his reach. It only required patience and a good temper. He wouldn't even have to move much around the sheds, as it sufficed to spend the whole shift in his office, morning or night; the drivers had to come to his office and leave the ignition key and their daily report sheet. His father got him his promotion and he stayed there for a long time. Ferenc Kolunga's son was happy among the trams. He came to love them. When Fanny and I were in Prague in the mid-eighties, we walked down Béla Bartók Avenue (whose string quartets are my favorite pieces of music) and passed a man in a tram driver's uniform who walked with the help of sticks in Zsigmont Móricz Square tram station) I don't remember his face, because I only saw him from the back, and for a few seconds at that, as he was disappearing through a door into an area that was off limits to non-authorized personnel. It was then that I began to imagine Hurbinek had survived.

3

The life of Pablo Orgambide

Or else:

Like Kolunga, Pablo Orgambide, the writer, was handed over to the Red Cross in Auschwitz without a name (or with that strange moniker of Hurbinek) and, just like Farin's or Kolunga's, his life could be Hurbinek's. Today I imagine him on his wedding day: it is a day at the end of November 1975 and Pablo is thirty-three. Two weeks before, a street boy killed Pasolini on the beach in Ostia and Pablo worshipped Pasolini. He is getting married in Madrid, in a country that is experiencing political upheaval under a moribund dictator who signed his last five death sentences a month before. A country that isn't *his*, though Pablo doesn't know that, and when, with the passage of time, there is overwhelming evidence that his real name was something else, it is to seem unimportant, because he has lived a life rich in experience with a name he has been known by ever since he can remember: Pablo Orgambide. They never told him, or made the slightest hint. How he came to be part of that family is a mystery, even for his family. His father, who gave him the name he now lives under and was the only one who knew the secret, died in 1968 and took it with him to the grave, and his mother had died many years before with her lips sealed: she had given birth to three daughters and that boy was to be be the son she couldn't give him. Then somebody, who perhaps wanted to spread doubts and wreak conflict between him and his sisters, circulated the rumor that their father had brought a child with him from Russia, when they began to allow men who had fought in the Blue Division to return. A child who surely was Pablo. He studied Law at the university where he joined a left-wing party that was clandestine at the time. When Franco was in his final death throes, Pablo enjoyed a comfortable position in society, though his family wasn't well-to-do, but merely middle class and fallen on hard times. Old man Orgambide, politically conservative and close to the Franco regime, worked as a lawyer in Spain for a Belgian timber company, the Compagnie Nationale des Bois, that owned land in the Congo. The Nationale lost its licence to operate and went bankrupt in 1956. It was the same year that Pablo began to write a weekly society column for the evening newspaper *Informaciones* where he met the woman he would marry, Esther Rubio. Pablo Orgambide now works for publishers in Barcelona who pay him quite well to write biographies of historical figures. He is thinking of giving the column up to continue with the series on a freelance basis and take on others as they come up. Coincidentally one of the biographies he finished before his wedding, in the summer of 1975, was Adolf Hitler's. (I think: it's really a macabre irony that Hurbinek should write a life of Hitler, but there was also a hint of vengeance.) He had gone to Majorca to finish the book. His fiancée's family owned a very rustic cabin that was called precisely that, Sa Cabana, on the road to Inca. He spent three months surrounded by books on the Third Reich and all kinds of apologias for the Führer. He ended up disgusted, because he thought that character was completely obnoxious. He found his hatred of the Jews abominable. And yet it was never revealed to him how close to that abomination he had in fact lived. When Pablo was in puberty and asked why that number was tattooed on his arm, he would only receive evasive replies, the sincere fruit of ignorance: nobody in the Orgambide family suspected the boy's real origins. "Don't tell us you are a Jew!" his sisters exclaimed scornfully, though in an incredulous rather than wary tone. His father got a number tattoo as well so he could tell his son it was an ancient family rite, a numbering that affected various members of the family over generations, an absurd explanation that Pablo accepted, as yet another of the strange ideas that ruled the impenetrable mind of his father, whom he admired but didn't understand however much the two of them took frequent strolls together along the streets of Madrid in an illusory attempt at sharing affection. Over time, his marriage to Esther would become a stable, happy union, because he found she supported him in his aspiration to be a writer, one that he did in fact fulfill. He wrote novels, history books, and still more biographies (his *Life of Hernán Cortés* became a classic; his biography of Hitler went through several editions and can even be found to this day on book bargain shelves, where I bought mine; he also wrote a life of Cervantes) and wrote fewer and fewer articles as a journalist until he finally gave up from exhaustion. He and Esther were to have two children.

He was to win prizes and collect aquariums with exotic fish, small, elusive fish, and that was to become his favorite hobby, as it was Primo Levi's when he was a child, when he named each fish after a mineral. But Orgambide died never knowing that they were together, even if only for a very short time, in Auschwitz. Travelling was never a problem, since that limp of his, that only weighed on him when he forgot to conceal it, never stopped him from leading the life he wanted to lead. Neither Esther nor he (come to think of it, he was fated to marry a woman whose name was so significantly Hebraic) thought the rumors about Pablo's Russian origins were in any way credible. Had they investigated further, those origins would have taken them to very distant places, a world that no longer existed but that once had as a backdrop a city called Rzeszów. The day I am imagining today, the day they wed, Franco died. He was asked to write Franco's life, but never did. Instead, he wrote a life of Pasolini.

4

The life of Paul Roux

Or else:

Paul Roux. Originally Polish but naturalized in France. He doesn't know what his name used to be or which city he was born in. He is only sure that he put in a sudden appearance, as if he'd fallen from the skies, in an orphanage in Alsace, that he left in order to enter a seminary of the Brothers of La Salle in Paris. He became very religious, a feature of his personality he never lost, not even when he gave up his vocation to devote himself fleetingly to the cinema. He met Georges Annenkov, the old friend and tailor of Ophuls and Renoir, by chance in a hotel, who introduced him into those circles. He played secondary roles in films directed by Sautet, Bresson, Truffaut, Clément and Chabrol. In the early eighties Susanne Lepape crossed his path. A cheerful, witty woman, she was shortish, robust and full of charm, and owned an opticians in Marseille that supplied lenses to the Gaumont production company. Susanne, like Paul, loved the cinema. They married and Paul began to work in his wife's business. He left Paris for a life in the provinces and never regretted it. Paul is a good man with simple tastes who likes a tranquil life, and Susanne enjoys the small things of life, the "small everyday pleasures" as she calls them. But together they nurture the passion that unites them: the cinema. On every anniversary, whether it be their wedding, respective birthdays or some personal occasion—given that any is a good excuse to give presents—they give each other items related to their common passion. Paul and Susanne are fetishists and cultivate an extraordinary, irrepressible taste for small myths. Thus they have given each other as presents a gold chain that belonged to Jean Marais (Paul), mother-of-pearl eyeglasses that were Romy Schneider's (Susanne), an almost new white bootee that belonged to Arletty (Paul), one of Alain Delon's handkerchieves embroidered with the initials A. D. (Susanne) and a Renoir zoetrope plus the original screenplay of *Les portes de la nuit* signed by Jacques Prévert (Paul) and Clouzot's amber cigarette case (Susanne). Valuable items, increasingly sought after by collectors. Year after year, the Rouxs' tastes become more sophisticated and they now have to go to auctions or involve intermediaries who sell objects belonging to famous actors and directors through the back door. However, Paul Roux's greatest fetish, one he longs to possess every twilight when he shuts the opticians and takes a stroll through the port of Marseille—the city that Walter Benjamin dreamed was being transformed into a book—and gazes at the yachts moored there, is *Marge*, Maurice Ronet's yacht in *À plein soleil*. He plays a small role in the final scenes of that film shot in a fishing port on the Adriatic. His love of boats is an impossible love: they are unattainable for him.

I am afraid Paul Roux doesn't know who Walter Benjamin was and hasn't read any of his books. That's why he doesn't know that early in the morning of September 27, 1940 he committed suicide in Portbou fleeing from the Nazis. He would have ended up in a train heading toward Auschwitz. He might have been gassed on arrival, or might have lived long enough to get to know little Hurbinek, to breathe the same pestilent air in that infirmary and die when some anonymous person rescued that child from death so he could become Paul Roux, former actor and optician, bringing them together historically, in a terrible, magnificent museum, a mountain of lost names, of deceased, displaced people, an artificial mountain of encounters and non-encounters.

The Rouxs don't have children and like to travel through Europe, and they celebrate their love in their journeying. Susanne drives since Paul has a few problems with his legs, where he lost a great deal of sensitivity, though he doesn't know when or how. Quite simply, he was born that way. But he holds himself up well, and does remember that he used a walking stick in the La Salle Seminary. Whenever they can, they go to the cinema or tirelessly watch films on video, and when they go up to Paris they visit their old friends: Léaud, Chabrol and Denner. In 1982 Susanne is to give him a present, the brooch in the form of a silver arrow that Joan Bennett wears on her beret in *Man Hunt*. It cost her a fortune, but it will make Paul happy. She was to give it to him in a hotel in Portbou, where they were to stop to break up their journey to Barcelona, on a special fictitious anniversary, when Paul was to turn forty. Or that was what they chose to believe. "But where were you born, Paul, what was the town?" No one knows.

5

The life of Ribo Varelisy

Or perhaps:

In April 1982, the famous Bulgarian conductor Ribo Varelisy, while on tour in Italy, made an unexpected request of the Uffizi Museum in Florence. He did so via a formal letter requesting permission to spend each night of his five days in the city in one of the rooms in the museum, specifically, the one displaying Boticelli's *Birth of Venus* (the greatest work of art ever created by man, in his opinion). He thought they should equip the room in a particular way for his overnight stays. They should provide bed and blankets and perhaps a basin. He made it clear he wasn't referring to the cubbyholes for security guards and room attendants, or the museum's administrative offices, but the exhibition rooms where paintings were hung and visited by the general public. He acknowledged that he was suffering from a kind of incurable pathology, one rather neglected by psychiatrists, in which the patient, when suffering anxiety attacks, needed to live in a museum or places with similar characteristics. He added that the pathology was known as shut cage syndrome. Ribo Varelisy suffered a crisis on that tour, one he described as among the worst in his life, and that was the reason for such an extraordinary request. To justify his eccentricity, Ribo Varelisy maintained he was in Auschwitz as a child—though his memory was blank on the subject—and as a result of the harsh conditions he was forced to endure they amputated his legs from mid-thigh down. He moves around in a motorized wheelchair, like a little car, and is world famous because he is the only orchestra leader on the planet who conducts seated thus.

6

The life of Augustus Hubbard

Or else this other possibility:

The following scene takes place in Bangkok, Thailand, three years after they opened the doors of the most famous museum in Florence to Varelisy as if it were a hotel. Now Hurbinek might be a botanist, a conservationist in Kew Gardens, a man by the name of Augustus Hubbard, whose real profession was that of art valuer, and who is to find out his true origins in 1985. Hubbard had travelled extensively around Asia over the last fifteen years as an agent prospecting for the Antiquities Department of Sotheby's. His profession, in which Gus—as everyone calls him—is a distinguished authority, has little or nothing to do with botany, Hubbard uses it as a front because it gives him access to houses, villages, plantations and ruins on the excuse that he is searching for a specific flower or vegetable that he wishes to study. That's why his visiting card says AUGUSTUS HUBBARD – SPECIALIST IN ASIAN BOTANY, KEW GARDENS. The works of art he is obliged to discover and catalogue for his firm, that are sometimes camouflaged as crude deities in hovels in Tibet or as domestic utensils in Vietnam, find a growing market in Europe. He heads the Asian commercial section of the hundred-year-old English antiques auctioneers. He doesn't do this by himself, as is obvious to anyone who knows anything about Gus Hubbard, since he cannot lift his feet off the ground, and walks or drags himself along very clumsily, as if he were wearing lead shoes or very large sizes of footwear. He has assembled a team of helpers, two Englishmen, a Burmese, a Philippine, and a Taiwanese woman, who do the selection work for him. Gus Hubbard considers himself to be an unusual offshoot of those Californian gold diggers. He is obsessive, always in pursuit of a jewel that is unique of its kind, like a pristine Ming vase, or a Mogul terracotta from the tomb of Genghis Khan, or an ivory screen from Kyoto, or one of the Buddha's eighty books of prophesy, or Japanese netsukes or sumptuous gold Siamese tapestry from Chiang Mai. Meanwhile, his team finds minor items that are much less fascinating, even commonplace, but that can nevertheless pass as highly valuable because they are so authentic. They fetch high prices in London auctions. Gus keeps his headquarters in Hong Kong, where he has lived all these years, but travels frequently to big cities in the region: Delhi, Calcutta, Singapore, Shanghai, Tokyo, Taiwan, Manila . . . He is a business man who looks like an explorer and the best way to define him would be as a laboratory analyst or a *maître d'*. Because Gus has nothing of the adventurer about him, quite the contrary in fact: he is short and thin, sweats, breaths asthmatically, is short-sighted and quite unappealing. He has never worried about his looks, truth be known, since his passion, ever since he can remember, although he is an adoptive son, has been Asia, and what he has succeeded to do in life is to travel there extensively, to get to know it in depth. And his body has never been an obstacle in that regard. One cannot say he has never enjoyed what life has to offer. No pleasure slips from his grasp; he loves every minute that passes as if some subconscious sense were telling him that everything around him and everything that happens to him exists in a web of time that is a gift, a time that no longer belongs to him, because there was another era when he was dead and part of a nightmare of History which few, very few managed to wake up from and forget. And that is something that Gus discovered today in Bangkok at the luxurious Oriental Hotel, opposite the sloops and motor boats that ply up and down the Chao Phraya River. His high bedroom windows have turned iridescent in the twilight glow from the Noi railroad station. It's warm and Gus is relaxing after a day spent evaluating remains from small temples in Kanchanaburi. He is listening to the radio, but hearing nothing: somewhere in the Atlantic they have found the real remains of the *Titanic*. Thousands of miles from there, in the Polish city of Rzeszów, Raca Cèrmik, a woman who is almost a hundred, can now die knowing where her beloved brother Thomas Zelman is resting. But why should that interest Gus Hubbard? A young waitress has brought him something for supper. Gus doesn't try even a mouthful; he sips whisky while he reads a long letter he has anxiously been expecting. You can hear the noise of the aeroplanes making their descent to the airport. When they pass overhead, the music from the Rim Room, the elegant nightclub on the opposite bank of the river, wafts up to his room. The street lights in China Town glow in the distance, against a black background of tall skyscrapers. He has found out from his step-brothers who've been investigating their true identity for several years, at Gus's expense. He is now holding the long letter from John, his elder brother, in which he tells him about Auschwitz, a place that he, Gus, could never have imagined was linked to his life (or, in fact, to his death, I would suggest). He then mentions a Russian soldier, a frightened young man from Simferopol, in the Crimea, as they discovered. He goes on to talk about a sick, paralytic child at death's door; and of a black market, just after the war ended, in morphine, of barter, of sales, of an Englishman who sells morphine in that black market among mutually repelling allies who are Russians and Englishmen, disgusted by a frightened Russian morphine addict who is about to kill a child by putting his hand over his mouth, of an Englishman who is a doctor who offers the Russian from Simferopol the morphine he is demanding in exchange for the life of a child who is dead already, of an English doctor who kept that child with him without giving him too much thought. A Polish child. No doubt a Jewish child. "Look at your arm, and draw your own conclusions," ends the letter from John Hubbard. What Gus had always thought of as the incomprehensible features of a whimsical tattoo, turned out to be numbers that were hardly legible even if you stretched the skin. Night is falling in Bangkok and suddenly he has ceased to be Augustus Hubbard, art valuer.

7

The life of Icek Bienenfeld

This Israeli photographer of Polish origin became notorious in the most liberal sectors of his country's society in the sixties, when he wrote comic strips for the *Jerusalem Post* under the pseudonym of Norman. He satirized Golda Meier and Moshe Dayan with caricatures that reversed their most obvious traits: he made Dayan seem very fat with a moveable bun on the top of his head, and his Meier wore a patch over one eye. However, Bienenfeld soon got bored of that and opened a photography studio in the new part of Jerusalem. His camera has taken photos of all the most renowned Israelis and many official photos carry his signature. One day in 1992—he remembers it was very early because he was in a bad mood and unable to utter a word, and that may be why it was the best time for her to choose—his wife told him she was divorcing him. Lena left him for another man, although she didn't make it that clear at the time. He was a cardiologist, Ariel Kreptchuk, but Icek only found that out later. To begin with, she went to live with Sonia, a friend, with whom Icek had had an affair. Fifteen years ago, for God's sake! He soon found that he was fifty—he only later fully realized—with a life as full as his house, with piles of possessions, and a future it was better not to burden with too many deadlines. He smoked and he coughed. Tobacco had taken many of his good friends in the neighborhood to the other side, and he, a man whose lungs had been damaged by tuberculosis and pneumonia as a child, had purchased, with excessive foresight, tickets in the raffle for cancer. And had bought them in abundance, what with the forty plus cigarettes he smoked a day. Perhaps that is why, when he'd assimilated the news of his divorce (Lena was much younger than he was, and had realized that her role from then on would be to fill in the cracks in the boat before it sank and had thus opted to re-make her life, since their love was marooned in the stagnant waters of the past), Bienenfeld burned all the photos he had of Lena, even those he had of them as a couple together, sold their house, split the money with her and decided to set out on a journey he had been deferring and never found an opportunity to undertake. "Out of insecurity, or fear, because I'm one of those birds that thinks that the forest floor is up there." He put himself on a passenger list held by a travel agency, Shalom, that offered tours around Europe with a variety of itineraries. Almost all began or finished in Barcelona, because of that year's Olympic Games, but others were very different, with visits to some of the concentration camps: Dachau, Buchenwald, Mathausen . . . Auschwitz. He chose the last one because he knew it was the place

139

where he had been born twice. "That's literally the truth: my mother and the Russians," he told me. He remembers nothing of either; perhaps with the help of pyschoanalysis he might have extracted from the pit of memory a great gray cloud of suffering, as gray as the Zyklon B produced by Farben, since that was all there had been to his childhood, suffering and more suffering. His mother? His father? His grandparents? His brothers, sisters, uncles, aunts and cousins? Did they ever exist? "They are as real as a set of prints of the Crusades!" he would say. These questions had buzzed around his head for years but never found a possible answer. He barely managed to establish that his family origins were Polish. He liked to think they came from Warsaw because he liked people who were born there. Someone who had survived told him that he might perhaps be a child of a family that had immediately been scattered around the camp, some gassed and others tortured. Bienenfeld was sure that fellow had got it wrong, that he had mistaken his family for another, or at least had no proof of what he was affirming. And what proof would have been eloquent enough? But it was better than nothing, better to have one probable scenario, rather than a hundred unreal ones, as went one of the titles of the popular writer Sholem Aleichem, and the day he bought his ticket from the Shalom travel agency with stops—according to his itinerary—in Vienna – Munich – Amsterdam – Hamburg – Berlin – Warsaw – Krakow – Auschwitz – Prague and then back to Israel, he wagered on that remote possibility. Hurbinek was returning to Auschwitz and was returning by himself.

8

The life of Walter Hanna

Hurbinek was going to Auschwitz, but not anymore.

Now here we have Walter Hanna, fifty-nine years of age, an ironic, seductive radio journalist specializing in sports—football, boxing, and above all swimming—residing in Salonika, Greece, 15 Mitropoleos Street, in an attic from which one can see the White Tower (he has always lived there, they'll even put a plaque on the façade). Single and homosexual, he has lived his life alone but not isolated; he has shared his most recent life with a lover, the singer Dimitriou Mitarakis, who has just died. He was his only family, plus friends, dozens of friends, because Walter Hanna is a very sociable, charismatic man. He also discovered he has AIDS and hasn't long to live, "I have loved so much . . . " he silently consoles himself and is not afraid. "Those of us who survived the Nazis can never be frightened again," he liked to say, "and possess a mysterious durability." He has lived on the edge, true enough, and squeezed dry the boundaries of every transgression, perhaps because he thought that "mysterious endurability" made him immune. When Dimitriou died, he told him, "I have been very happy." He kissed him on the lips and added, "Thank you." But now in the spring of 2001 Walter Hanna is in a hospital, on the outskirts of Berlin. That is what he requested, almost insisted upon, he doesn't want to enter Berlin, he wants to be as far away as possible from

the Unter den Linden and Friedrichstrasse; *Deutschland,
Deutschland über alles,* that "Germany above all," echoes
around his head and gives him goose bumps; he remembers
that Joseph Roth, whom he reads and re-reads frequently,
had already said that no Jew went to Berlin of his own
free will. He is in the hospital because he has been in a car
accident, like me, when he was driving to Auschwitz. He
didn't mean to go through Berlin, but he'd been misled
several times by the German motorway signs and took the
wrong turn. The map in his rented car was no use, was too
old. Before he realized it, he was already twenty-five miles
from the capital, and any other route, back to Dresden or
down to Prague, would have have sidetracked him even
more. Then he skidded and crashed into a camper that was
parked on the hard shoulder. It's not serious, but they gave
him a blood test in hospital and confirmed what he already
knew. The medical report has the hint of a fatal diagnosis:
he is bleeding internally and it's dangerous to continue in
such state. "How strange," he thought, "it's as if they were
sentencing me to death here, yet again, fifty years later."

He was always Jewish and always lived among Jews.
The Sephardis of Salonika, savagely reduced after the war,
welcomed him as they did so many thousands who came
from the camps and were on their way down to Palestine.
He was in a truck full of moribund children. Only five were
saved, and he was one, and nobody remembered his real
name, so he gave himself the one he has now when it was
time to go into the army, perhaps because he liked Walter
Rogas, an Italian sporting journalist. He was declared unfit
for service because his legs were shorter than normal.
Now that he knows his end is near, he decided to go to

Auschwitz and confront his destiny, face the inevitable pilgrimage to that kernel of History. But now finds himself in a German hospital, unable to move, and at the mercy of ghosts. Hurbinek will never make it to Auschwitz. At least for a second time.

Nevertheless there is something that is still possible, an absurd hope: that Walter Hanna, the journalist whose voice in Greece is as famous as Melina Mercouri's, is *really* inhabiting the same present as myself, the very same day, the very same hour as I imagine him, not very far away, in another German town, both of us simultaneously in hospital. And it could be absolutely for real, it could be true that at the very moment when I am rescuing Hurbinek from the dead and giving him a life, the real Walter Hanna, or whatever his name is, is there, in that hospital, because he was *really* born in Auschwitz and had *really* made the journey, his life's last, that far. Then Hurbinek had certainly lived *über alles*, above all else, as the hymn goes.

VIII

TWO WORDS OR PERHAPS ONE

1

Henek has got up and attuned his ears to try to catch the words apparently coming out of Hurbinek's mouth.

For several days the child has been uttering a sound that is incomprehensible to those surrounding him in the barrack. In fact, they are two words—*mass-klo, matisklo*—or perhaps just one, the variations introduced by his hoarse, agonizing breathing. Patzold, who first mistook them for Bohemian vowels, is reminded of Latin declinations, with their different endings and suffixes, and consequently imagines Hurbinek to be Romanian in origin, though as far as he knows there are very few Romanians in the camp.

In that cold, dark February, Henek, sitting on one side of the child's bed—a sort of cradle he himself made—observes the small bulk that is Hurbinek, who cannot curl up because his legs have gone dead, and crosses Hurbinek's hands over his chest, in a position straining to retain heat, where his breath can reach them, though he shivers constantly.

Henek strokes the woollen hat with ear flaps they have given him. Hurbinek's gaunt, dirty face, that seems even more gloomy in the dim light filtering through the cracks from outside, sways rhythmically on a pillow stuffed with straw. He looks more like a doll than a child. Henek listens attentively, tirelessly, to the language of his protégé.

He thinks there are two words, one ending in *as* and the other in *o*. Some, like Primo Levi or Franz Patzold, argue they can only hear one, one spoken hesitantly, uttered inevitably haltingly because of his gasps, as if he had hiccups (hence the sudden separation of the two syllables or aspirated *tis* sound). Sometimes Henek hears *maschs glo* and at others claims that the second word, transformed into *blo* and then *klo* is repeated twice or three times, with the syllables switching place: *blo - klo - blo - klo*. The boy might even be saying three words: *mass* [maschs] *blo klo*. And these three words belong to the refrain of a lullaby rather than a sentence with any meaning. They remind Henek remotely of the words of a lullaby he knows, although he is sure the words aren't Hungarian. He explained that to everyone, when, as well as asking how many words little Hurbinek is uttering, they wonder what they might mean. Henek felt they were very similar to "the mill wish woosh" he recalled in a dialect ditty sung by peasant women in the Beskides, a lullaby children repeated, imitating the sounds animals and objects make on a farm.

dar ruk ko ko
dar bletz crep crep
dar maschs blu blo

[*cock doodle doo*
fire crackle crackle
mill wish woosh]

Ernst Sterman thought Hurbinek was trying to say his name, but when had he ever learned such a thing? As for Scholomo Buczko the cobbler, he was simply whimpering like a sick baby animal. For others, like Rubem Yetzev, the word spoken by Hurbinek was simply a word of affection he had repeatedly heard at intervals in his short life, a kind of "duck," "luvvie" or "darling" or just "my little one," said by someone, perhaps his mother, or by whoever picked him up and saved him and brought him there where, alone and lost, he was clinging to a survival that seemed increasingly unlikely. For school master Yetzev they were the only warm, loving words Hurbinek had heard in his short little life, words whispered by a trembling voice, in danger, at a decisive moment, that he now repeated like a small animal stiff with cold and fear, hoping to hear the affectionate tone of that protective voice that had taught him them before disappearing. The psalm-like insistence with which Hurbinek said those words in all his suffering was but his instinctive expression of despair and anguish.

Gradually, as days went by, they all became increasingly obsessed by those short words. They were fascinated by their ambiguous, indefinable meaning. Each individual detected the meaning he wanted to hear for himself: some longed for songs from their childhood, other recalled the innocence of their early years or were transported by melancholy to a moment when they were happy, one of those moments that is as hard as a rock and rushes back

147

into the memory like a lost paradise that, when times are bad, can prop up an entire life. Each of them, in the foul-smelling barrack, thought of a moment in the past that was frozen in time, abstracted from history, when they experienced the happy eternity they so longed for, a state of stillness, a premature but sweet anticipation of death.

In the words of Hurbinek, everyone began to want to utter a language of their own, a language without past or present, or at any rate without the past they abandoned as the greatest exercise in horror a human being could ever suffer. They all wanted to remove themselves from that place and time and fly off on the gurgles made by that moribund baby to a life of quiet elsewhere, that would preserve them in a bubble of the most elemental bliss, that relates every feeling and moment of warmth to the maternal bosom.

The dirty blankets covering Hurbinek are his real language. In his heart of hearts, Henek, the extreme realist, understands that with a survivor's keen common sense stripped of metaphor. And that contradiction between lullaby or loving whisper, as absent from Auschwitz as the sun is from the night and the filth all around, makes Henek weep in the early morning, when dawn's icy light brings a tinge of blue to the excrement from patients with dysentery that is dotted throughout the barrack. By his side Hurbinek grates his gritted teeth: he wasn't asleep. His large eyes were simply entering a state of lethargy in which his gasps blotted out the slightest sound he articulated, but Henek knew that wasn't a dream, only an extreme point of exhaustion in Hurbinek's hurried search for an answer to his requests, expressed in that clumsy, inchoate language.

Reality, like pain, made its mark once more during those weeks: someone died (Abrahan Levine, from diphtheria, cared for as best he could by Rubem Yetzev); some extracted food from the Polish nurses and others waited in their beds, trying to recover the strength that had deserted them. Hurbinek's words thus became one more element in that reality, transfigured nonetheless into a symbol of what those men were experiencing. That obsessed them for a month: deciphering, understanding, interpreting those three miserable, enigmatic, barely audible words, because they knew they might be the only words possible at such a time, at that precise moment.

Those able to move took shifts night and day by the side of Hurbinek's bed, hoping that the Word, just one, might be revealed in all its purity, that would allow them to surrender to him and save their life. And be saved, thanks to that word they surmised but never heard, or at least that was what some—Berek Goldstein or Chaim Roth—imagined. Hurbinek became for many an extraordinary Messiah in a process of silent self-immolation.

In a way, those men depended on the language imposed by Hurbinek, since at the end of the day they unconsciously began to think that those words expressed what they themselves wanted to say though they realized to their astonishment they never did; words that enclosed ambiguous meanings, like the periods in Chemistry for Primo Levi, and sought a way out to reach the name from the world of the unnameable: "hunger" or "fear" or "bread" or "heat," or perhaps a blind, deep, elemental demand for an explanation via a robust verb the young boy could never find; at best or above all, those words merely wanted to ask "why?" And that was why they snatched at scraps of knowledge in childish verse or the most primeval "I love you." They were returning to that primitive, primary language for urgently naming fear, desire or dire necessity.

That language sank them all in silence. It was one paradox produced by the sight of Hurbinek. For a month they barely spoke if it wasn't to refer to him; they only responded to the sounds that child made, sounds that immediately vanished, the prescient symptom of an intense, humiliating wail. A dirty silence, as dirty and silent as streets were now, and houses, bodies, mathematics, novels, trombones, newspapers, and the dead throughout Europe.

Henek strains to listen to Hurbinek's voice. He brings his lips close to his cheek. He knows it is a privilege. "Hello, my little sweet," Sofia Pawlicka, Cèrmik by her maiden name, would have said, in other circumstances, had she been alive.

2

Some words belong to a dream.

Walter Benjamin had a dream on June 28, 1938. He was climbing a ladder but couldn't see the top. Other ladders like his were everywhere, that other people were climbing. They took a long time; they were very steep at the end. The ladder came to a sudden halt and he saw he had reached the top, a fragile step separating him from the void. He looked around and saw other men in the same situation, at the top of their respective peaks. One raised his hand to his head and said, "I am dizzy and feel sick" and hurtled down from the peak. That dizziness spread and they fell one after another, after they'd raised their hands to their foreheads. When Benjamin felt dizzy symptoms—or thought he did in his sleep—he woke up.

And I have just woken up from a similar dream in the hospital in Frankfurt: in my dream I was on the top of a mountain of rubbish and filth. I couldn't identify the kind of rubbish, but I knew, *as a matter of course*, that it was foul-smelling; there were old clothes, scrap metal and even human remains that I accepted, *as a matter of course*. Next to me, at the top of the mountain, someone had nailed up a sign: FRANKFURT. From where I stood, I could see two other mountains, also containing all manner of filth and rubbish. The sign on one said AUSCHWITZ and on the other WARSAW. There was a man like myself on both peaks, deaf in fear and shock. *I knew* that both men were me, but they didn't have my face. Then one of them, the furthest away, (WARSAW), sank into his mountain, *as a matter of course*, and was swallowed up by the detritus. The other man and I stared at each other, but as we did so, the second was also swallowed up by his mountain (AUSCHWITZ). The nurse woke me up because I was waving my arms and was soaked in sweat. She was afraid I had a temperature and gave me an injection, but when I came round and she left the room, I couldn't get to sleep again. The cold presence of the nurse reminded me that I was still in Frankfurt, and I thought of Benjamin. I thought how I was in the city that had allowed Mengele to qualify as a doctor, yet hadn't accepted Benjamin as a teacher in Goethe University. Benjamin wrote that some kinds of important dreams endure in the shape of certain words.

I wonder which word would contain his dream of the men falling from their mountain peaks. Perhaps it was simply that word: peak, or maybe dizziness, and hence, the end, and hence, and why not? revenge. In my case, the word that encapsulates my dream is paralysis. I was going to Auschwitz, but not anymore. Or the word is shit, and hence origin, and terror.

What dream did Hurbinek's words belong to?

With one finger, Henek lovingly cleans the dribble from the boy's lips and listens. Henek listens every day, Henek listens every night.

3

After the horror, dumbness is all, and Hurbinek was dumb. His words—if that is how one can describe those syllables that emerge from his mouth, like the sigh from a disenchanted angel who lets himself drift into death, and not the projections from the men around him in this shack for the sick—his words were simulacra of an elemental language as unutterable as a sacred or accursed name.

There are words that are not possible.

Jean Améry wrote in one of his books, "Words cease in any place where a reality is imposed that is totalitarian in form." Améry was in Auschwitz and survived. He discovered what "totalitarian in form" meant in its purest state, where death was gratuitous and life was worthless. He had coincided with Primo Levi in the Buna-Monowitz factory, but they didn't meet then. Améry's real name was Hans Mayer and he was from Vienna. He changed his name in 1938 when he sought refuge in Belgium. But here's another throw of the dice by fate: by chance he chose the name of John Amery, son of the former British Minister of War and founder of the Legion of St. George, a military society created to support the Nazis at the heart of Great Britain. Did he ever realize? Maybe not. It is irrelevant, perversely curious. John Amery was hung by the Allies, and Jean Améry, like Primo Levi, committed suicide. He took an overdose of barbiturates in a Salzburg hotel in 1978, after mercilessly pouring scorn on the word-mongering of poets who were friends of the Nazis, like Ernst Bertram and Gottfried Benn. Benjamin said that as we get older words make more of an impact, and even a single word, however impossible it may seem, can impact so strongly it can lead to a new, even definitive state of mind. Perhaps the word Améry found was the same one that Hurbinek uttered: the desperate attempt to voice silence. Or the lost line from the lullaby sung by the peasant women in the Beskides mountains that Henek had sung. After the horror, only dumbness can ensue.

4

Henek makes an effort. I admire the effort he makes to do things. Like, for example, getting Hurbinek to speak. He spends a lot of time by his side, teaching him to pronounce his name, Hurbinek, a name that isn't even his real one, a name they've all given him there, after Henek interpreted a few vague sounds, the almost guttural noises the child made, and suggested that name quite persuasively because

153

they suddenly reminded him of the name of a footballer he once met who played for Ferencváros.

"He got out of a car in my town and said hello to everyone. And shook my hand."

When Henek comes back from flirting with the nurses (or them with him, particularly Jadzia, the thin, anemic Polish nurse who'd been tortured and didn't dare touch Hurbinek and when she did so, she couldn't avoid showing her repugnance), he spends hours caressing the arms of the child so they don't get cold and tenderly spelling out his name in syllables, "Hur-bi-nek, Hur-bi-nek, Hur-bi-nek."

Again and again, and with an insistence for a lost cause the rest of the men in the barrack had never seen before. Every day, while Hurbinek was alive, Henek sat by his side and patiently repeated his name. He was loathe to accept, after pronouncing those syllables, just as he'd heard them, that in fact the child was only emitting a sound of pain or sorrow.

But Hurbinek never said Hurbinek, in spite of all that.

Henek understood the nurses reasonably well. He mixed up words from the languages he had heard in the camp: Yiddish, Hungarian, Polish, plus a couple of greetings in Russian, sexual obscenities in Slovakian, three ways of saying "don't forget me" and "I hate you" in Greek, and the odd German word, like *mensch*, "fellow," that was forever on his lips as an epithet for anything.

Thanks to that mosaic of languages he managed to find food and clean clothes for the sick in the shack, particularly for Hurbinek, who immediately dirtied himself and never had the right clothing—his body shrunk so rapidly by the day, and he was so worn down at the end, when he died, that his shroud consisted of a trouser leg and half a blanket. Consequently the words that began to be more habitual around him appertained to material objects, were all concrete and real: shirt, blanket, bowl, spoon, cap, shit, water, bread, morphine, hair, cudgel, rat, eye. Henek repeated them ten, twenty times, when he had the opportunity, so he would learn—"My shirt, shirt, shirt," and pointed to his clothes, "Your cap, cap, cap" and touched what he was wearing on his head. "Water, water, water" and made him drink from a tin. "Your eye, eye, eye" and put his finger on Hurbinek's cheek.

Sometimes Henek tried to teach him words he had heard the executioners use, such as *fressen*, that he used meaning "to eat" when in fact it meant "throw the pigs some feed" or "fodder" because that's what they were in the eyes of the SS, livestock, animals only kept alive to be slaughtered. Or *spritzen*, the favorite word of Höss, the Camp Commandant, who would repeat it to great laughter when they were slicing through a child's neck and the blood streamed down its body, "Spurt, spurt!" Patzold and Goldstein reproached Henek for using these words that were damned because they evoked a raft of painful experiences that they then re-lived. Primo Levi told them those meanings were degraded, were language that must be forgotten, erased from dictionaries, removed from all tongues, destroyed in books. "They are words that should be tried and executed," schoolmaster Rubem Yetzem would say in turn.

"*Wstawać!*"

Primo Levi relates how this Polish word was the word he most feared and hated, the one that pursued him in his nightmares for the rest of his life after January 1945. It was the dawn word, the word for waking up from a sleep into which your body collapsed exhausted, sleep that healed nothing, simply a paralyzing of life in motion where the torture of starvation surfaced in the subconscious, the only sleep really possible. It was a cruel word that carried within it an unpleasant sensation of cold and intense discomfort, reality that couldn't be eluded, non-sleep. He defined it as "the foreign order": "Get up!"

Henek hears that word no longer and similarly no one else in the camp hears it now. It has disappeared. But the tinny, absurdly nasal voice over the loudspeakers (when Henek heard the word "death" it would always remind him of the nasal loudspeaker in Auschwitz) still echoes in the ears of everyone and begins in the middle of the night. It is easy to mistake Hurbinek's coughs for the howls from that loudspeaker: "*Raus! Raus!*"[3]

They take their time to become mere coughs in the head of Henek, who suddenly wakes up, eyes bulging out of their sockets and temples quivering. Frightened, he gets up in the night and seeks consolation by kissing and touching Hurbinek.

Then when he recovers his sense of absurd normality, Henek helps Hurbinek; a torture renewed every night; death zigzags across the anonymous child's straw cradle.

---

3 "Outside! Outside!"

He runs his hand over his back and presses the sores; the child produces an even wheezier rattle. What did he say? Henek wonders, but it isn't a word, only a word in disguise, a stammer, an intention that is never fulfilled. Hurbinek's eyes want to live and are glued to Henek's reactions. He repeats his two words, or perhaps one. *Mass klo*, very quietly. Sleepy Henek hasn't heard it.

"*Mass klo*" Hurbinek repeats making a supreme effort.

Henek brightened up when he heard that and understood he was asking him to stay there, where language and time had been suspended. He cuddled up to him and for the first time realized that Hurbinek's belly was going up and down very fast. That was his reply.

6

Are words eternal?

For almost fifteen years, the Führer's fetish word and the favorite word in Germany was *Vernichtung*, "annihilation." It was used as much as *auszurotten*, "eradicate." In the bed next to me, my companion in this hospital ward is reading these same words in a sporting newspaper. The German language has a very poor memory.

7

Walter Benjamin had a prophetic dream on September 10, 1939, a year before he died. He was sitting on the branch of a tree. Underneath him was a kind of lawn or green wooden dais and a huge crowd spread over a meadow on a hillside. They wandered about like zombies and lived in barracks that were aligned symmetrically; they all wore prison garb. They were skinny, and some repeated in their companions' ears "They will burn us, they will burn us." They looked up, to where he was sitting, but weren't looking at him, as he thought, but at a huge figure even higher up. It was a child in a general's uniform. He couldn't see his face but could make out his arm and his stripes. His arm made movements similar to a child putting his hand into a box of toys. Perching on his branch, he jotted down the most important ideas he'd ever had, and did so on sheets of paper that then drifted down onto the crowd. His tiny writing filled each sheet and left no margins. Those who read a sheet, ate it and looked back up. Were they perhaps expecting more? As if responding to the unvoiced question as to why he was writing those sheets, Benjamin replied loudly, "It is very spiritual," but the child in the general's uniform didn't respond, and put his head into the box the wood of the tree with the branch where he was sat had become. Everything seemed to indicate they would stay like that indefinitely—him writing, the people down below reading, then swallowing the sheet—when he discovered that the child was sick and was about to die. From his branch he heard the doctor say, "When he dies, shut the box and throw it on the fire." That horrified him so much he woke up. Who could have imagined that Benjamin's dream anticipated camps like Auschwitz or Treblinka? "I have had a frightful dream," he wrote to a friend, "but I don't know what it means."

Walter Benjamin was going to Auschwitz, but not anymore.

IX

STONES FULL OF VOICES

1

Place is all. Place creates reality. That's why I buy realities. That's why I buy places.

One cannot understand Auschwitz *in its totality* without knowing the place, without knowing the place *in its totality* by heart.

What is its climate like, what is the color of the soil, what is the snow like in Auschwitz, what sort of view does one get *from there*? The thousands of photos I've seen have never made me feel I am in that place.

What does one breathe in Auschwitz?

I buy memory. I buy the lot, that is, I buy that climate, that soil, and that air. The location, in a word. I am a desperate, alert buyer in this Frankfurt hospital room.

I will visit the Auschwitz camps—now called Oświęcim once again—in Poland; of course I will; I will visit them later, in the cold month of March. I will succeed in what I have failed so far. Perhaps I really will some day, I tell myself, but not now (my body is in so much pain, my legs are still sheathed in plaster, I so badly need to leave this country whose history is like a throbbing migraine!) I will visit the Auschwitz camps in due course, will go on a tourist package with lots of Jews, Italians, and two or three Spaniards, but no Germans (evidently, Germans never visit Auschwitz—statistics don't lie), I will accompany the group to the entrance over which one can read the undulating letters—an imitation of a strip of cloth—and the cruelly ironic slogan *Arbeit Macht Frei*, "Work Makes You Free"— the motto for all the camps ever since someone inscribed it in the first, Dachau-1933—and I will see the railroad tracks, and then, inevitably, the truncated brick chimney, all that remains that seems genuinely sinister, though abstract as if it were an object out of context. Everything here is out of context, I will reflect as I walk over the paving in the camp, stones full of voices that are heard by very few, that are heard by me. Whispered voices more like. Crazed voices. Voices that are suddenly silenced, struck by real blows that split open skulls or break jaws.

The place is now only an empty space, a uniformly flat, snow-covered plain where one can see the silhouettes of distant lines of barracks and barbed wire fences with lamps shaped like butchers' hooks, hanging intact on concrete posts, nightmarish adornments memory imprints on its wax against oblivion, on behalf of the ghosts. That day I will have traveled the forty-five miles from Krakow and alighted from bus number 24, at the end of its route opposite the Auschwitz Museum, a few feet from the car park. Soon I will deliberately get lost, searching for Hurbinek's tree in the little forest of birchtrees surrounding Crematorium VI at the feet of which are hundreds of labels with names in Hebrew nailed on small stakes. Only ruins and gaping holes remain of the actual Crematorium.

Everything in Auschwitz is a gaping hole in something else that no longer exists.

Close by, covered in earth and weeds, are signs of several narrow gullies. Barely fifty years ago they were full of half burnt corpses because the ovens couldn't keep pace with demand.

This is what I shall see the day I go to Auschwitz.

2

The place. I need to refer to the place once again.

Oświęcim, the city in Upper Silesia, first Polish, then Austrian, then Polish again, then German, then finally back to Polish, is today a city with a population of 45,000 inhabitants: for some it is a tortured place, for others it is accursed. In 1939, when the Wehrmacht invaded Poland, it had 12,000 inhabitants, and an antiquated artillery barracks that surrendered without offering any resistance. Only a sergeant in the Polish army, by the name of Prohaska, died. A few months after Oświęcim was taken, Arpad Wigand, a colonel in the Security Police, visited on a fact-finding mission, carrying out orders from *SS Reichsführer* Heinrich Himmler, and he concluded he had found exactly the right place on the plain one could see from the barracks to build the large concentration camp for the East that they were planning in Berlin. Himmler was delighted with the report he received from Wigand and on April 27, 1940 he signed the decree for the camp to be built. In Wigand's view, as he noted in his report, the suitability of the place was based on the fact that it was a railroad junction, the Auschwitz-Birkenau station, reached by trains from Silesia, Czechoslovakia and Vienna, and from the cities in the East under the recent General Government, like Katowice, Krakow and Warsaw. It was also very easy to re-direct convoys there that were coming from the Ukraine and Byelorussia. Moreover, it had an added advantage: the Vistula and Sola Rivers flowed into each other in the nearby area of Broschkowitz, north-east of Birkenau, Brzezinka in Polish, thus creating a huge hairpin that isolated a large part of the region of Bielitz, under the administration of the city they now re-christened as Auschwitz. The camps were rapidly built and repeatedly extended between the two rivers.

3

The gas chambers were mostly set toward the north-east, in the area of Birkenau known as Auschwitz II.

The lethal Zyklon-B basically comprised cyanide acid, a gas concocted for the purpose of killing rats by its manufacturers, Degesch, a Frankfurt enterprise— Frankfurt yet again!—the diabolical city where I am now convalescing, the city I want to escape from but can't.

It was Camp Commandant Rudolf Höss, who found a new use for that gas. He had discovered it had been tested out in the spring of 1942 as an agent for exterminating Jews. It was a highly successful experiment. That summer Höss began to order thousands of cans of Zyklon-B from its distributors, two Hamburg firms, Tesch and Stabenow. All these firms prospered throughout those years and continued to exist after the war and even contributed to the "German economic miracle."

As many as 20,000 prisoners passed through the gas chambers daily. Two out of every three prisoners who got off the cattle trucks went straight to be gassed.

Men, women and children were stripped before they went in. They had no false expectations about where they were headed. Children consoled their parents.

Death from breathing in the gas wasn't immediate, but was terribly drawn out, people could take a minimum of five minutes and a maximum of twenty, even thirty, to die. The bodies writhed, then lay twisted and tangled on top of each other. It was a good forty minutes before they were removed, the time required to re-fill the chambers with fresh air.

4

I have seen a photo of Dr. Eduard Wirths. He joined the *Waffen SS* on his thirtieth birthday in 1939. The day the photo was taken, Wirths is doctor-in-chief, the *SS-Sturmbannführer* commandant, responsible for the sanitary area in Auschwitz: he is a gynecologist and expert in racial liquidation and sterilization, a friend of Mengele's and a special, close friend of Höss, the camp boss, with whom he shared a great fondness for horses. Wirths is smiling in that photo, is standing and looking at the photographer, posing with his hands clasped behind his back. It could be a perfectly innocent photo, taken in any field barracks anywhere on the front, if it weren't for the presence behind him of Crematorium IV operating at full strength, on a November day in 1942. Black smoke is coming out of the two square chimneys that leave macabre particles of soot floating in the air. Wirths is looking south, close to the window of the *Waffen SS*'s messroom near the kitchen and toilets. Barely sixty-five feet further on, to the east of this building, you can see the skylights of the room where people took their clothes off (used soon after as the dumping ground for the very same individuals who had stripped off there, whose corpses were piled up like sacks to facilitate the extraction of teeth before they were placed in the ovens), and a little further away, in the most distant section of that building, you get a glimpse in the photo of the sealed doors of the chambers. A man in his striped prisoner garb and wearing a cap is looking at the thin, tall, elegant, uniformed, haughty Wirths. He has just arrived from Norway to take up his new duties. He is wearing riding boots. He has promised Höss's mother, a childhood friend of Wirth's mother in Würzburg, that they will go for a ride every morning in the area around the Birkenau camp as far as the camp in Budy, the other side of the Harmense ponds, to the south-west of Auschwitz. A three or four miles ride in all to help put worries aside, even though his greatest worry is ending the outbreak of typhus now spreading everywhere. They must gas more people, burn them more quickly, the two riders comment as their steeds' hoofs ring out over the ground. Speed up, speed up, is the slogan. Fire destroys all evil. Höss's stables are different to the prisoners' barracks in that they are cleaner and well looked after, even bedecked with vases of flowers. Every morning Wirths himself changes the flowers. When he hung himself in September 1945 all they found in one of his pockets was a photo of him with Höss grooming his horse in one of the Auschwitz stables. He was held to be a good doctor. He killed two million Jews.

5

The ashes finally impregnate everything with their dark gray. They fall and settle like strange black snow. When an easterly wind blows, the inhabitants of houses in Auschwitz and Birkenau must shut their windows. The surface of brooks flowing from the Vistula and Sola slurp along under a thick, dirty-foam-like layer of ash. A lot of barbel and trout swallow this ash in the water. People sometimes eat this fish and think it's tasty, and why shouldn't they? The rain melds the ash into the soil on the farms. The porridge they feed to many of the prisoners, as well as the potato and cabbage soup with mutton eaten by the camp guards in the area of Auschwitz—that is Birkenau, Monowitz, Jawischowitz, Goleschau, Neu-Dachs, Budy and Blechhammer—the milk drunk by the inhabitants of the Bielitz region, from cows grazing on local pasture land, *everything* edible contains something of the ashes the Crematoria chimneys expel night and day. The region has descended into a new, unsuspected form of pandemic cannibalism.

Only the blind didn't see the ashes; nobody and nothing else could escape them.

When I spoke to Fanny and the girls a while ago, I could hardly keep myself upright on the crutches the nurse left me. It is not easy to coast along on legs in plaster-casts. I'll soon be leaving, I told them, one more week at most. Fanny offers to come and get me. I convinced her not to. What would be the point? Who went in search for Hurbinek, who went only to bring anyone back from Auschwitz? No one, and I don't want anyone to fetch me from here. What am I saying? How can I even compare myself . . . ? I'm on the mend, even though I run the risk of going mad in this Universitäts-Kliniken on Theodor Sternstrasse. They brought me these crutches. I can walk now, I practice a few steps every day, I venture out of my room and wander down the hallway. Someone from the Spanish Consulate paid me a visit the other day. A short, chubby guy who turned out to be the consul; he spent the whole time telling me about the sober, brown furniture in the Consulate, "in the late-fascist style of the thirties," he said, transported there in the days of Castiella. He insisted I should go and take a look before returning to Madrid. He assured me that almost all the furniture dates back to 1939, when Serrano Súñer was ambassador in Berlin on behalf of his brother-in-law Franco. The consul says Hitler always said how much he liked the furniture in the Spanish Embassy. Did he actually visit the place?

"Once, one July 18."

When the consul was leaving, he said, "You know, things last longer than we do."

The stones in Auschwitz came to mind.

7

At 10:30 a.m. on a Saturday in the autumn of 1944 Wirths landed in the aerodrome of Gleiwitz, some three hours away from Auschwitz. He was on his way back from Berlin, where he'd arrived the previous day, from the family estate in Baden-Baden. His mother had bought him a horse and he had gone to see it. Wirths called it *Auschwitz*. He also brought regards for Höss's mother from her son. When they said goodbye, no one could imagine that both they and Germany would be dead in less than a year.

He had breakfast at a checkpoint in the station in Biala. As he was eating, three train loads of prisoners came through on their way to Auschwitz. They did not stop.

He left at noon for Auschwitz.

At 1:00 p.m. he reached the camp and went to see Höss. When he arrived, they were unloading the third trainload onto the ramps on the Auschwitz 1 platform. The convoy had come from Hungary. All of those on the train were immediately taken to the gas chambers.

At 4:00 p.m. he went to the infirmary to sterilize four gypsy women. Two bled to death on their bunks. He issued the usual, pertinent orders for such cases.

At 5:30 p.m. he went to Crematorium III to personally supervise the cremation of the two gypsy women. He was very conscientious about his work. However, he didn't find them because their bodies had been mixed up with the 133 other bodies that were being gassed at the time.

At 6:10 p.m. he visited the camp stables and lingered for fifteen minutes feeding and grooming his horse.

At 7:00 p.m. he had dinner with other officers.

At 8:15 p.m. he listened to a Furtwängler recording of the *Meistersingers* in his bedroom.

At 8:30 p.m. he cleaned his pistol.

At 9:10 p.m. he fell asleep. By then they had already killed that day in the camp 185,302 prisoners. However, no one knew the precise number: the list of those eliminated wasn't exhaustive.

A year later the citizens of Baden-Baden ended up eating *Auschwitz*, the horse that his mother gave him as a present.

8

The camps in the area of Auschwitz-Birkenau alone occupied an area of 489 hectares. They built on that terrain 640 units for barracks, crematoria, gas chambers, housing for the SS garrison responsible for guard duties, rooms for officers, central command, workshops, hospitals, stores, punishment cells, water purifiers, factories, as well as the stables and the barracks for prisoners. The average number of prisoners housed at any time was 250,000. When the Red Army entered the camp there were only some 65,000. There were six crematoria, each equipped with 12 ovens, each one divided in turn into 45 sections. Each section could take five adult corpses, and took twenty minutes to burn a corpse. As they gassed people quicker than they could incinerate them, they also began to burn bodies in mass open graves, by sprinkling gasoline over the bodies. The smell spread several miles around. They used every means to manufacture the dead at top speed.

Two of those they killed were Sofia and Yakov Pawlicka.

9

I have always been afraid of going crazy. And so was Yakov Pawlicka, the father of Hurbinek who could never know he was his son. From childhood losing one's mind on the stage of history always seemed like an appalling fate. Like the man who went to Waterloo after becoming obsessed with reading *La Chartreuse de Parme* and wandered across the former battlefield thinking he was Fabrice del Dongo. Some people go to Waterloo as *Stendhalian* tourists, hunt for ghosts and mirages, and find them.

One cannot travel to Auschwitz in that frame of mind. It is neither right nor possible. But madness is never far away. I am thinking of the madness suffered by Yakov Pawlicka during those last weeks before he died, the mental fog where he lost himself before being taken to the gas chamber. He never discovered he had a son in Auschwitz. Better that way. His madness would have been compounded by the anguish caused by even greater suffering. Sofia never saw him again after they were separated on arrest. She was going to tell him that afternoon when they were arrested, she was going to tell him that she was pregnant, but she never had the slightest opportunity. When they got into the different trucks that were to take them to the concentration camps, their lives separated out for ever, and they would never meet again.

I sometimes think I will be better after this trip, but other times I think that when I reach Auschwitz I will be overwhelmed by the real madness of history, the madness of the horror, the madness of Yakov Pawlicka that hovers eternally over the camps of Auschwitz like air that is unbreathable. I even think that, when one doesn't travel as a tourist, one travels in search of self-improvement. And yet many people return with a lesser or greater degree of madness. But I am also sure there is a moral quest in every journey. I was going to Auschwitz, but not anymore. Perhaps the onset of my madness came prior to the journey and I should admit I was travelling in order to give Hurbinek's short life a second birth, as if I were a demiurge, through my gaze, by seeing what he saw. I will go to Auschwitz for that alone. It is an act of justice, although it may very likely be an act of madness as well.

10

However, there is another kind of madness. For example, Eduard Wirths helping his friend Rudolf Höss to write a letter-cum-report for Arthur Liebehens, the new camp commandant, who came from Majdanek in November 1943 to take over from Höss. That letter-cum-report glossed over everything to do with the day-to-day running of the camp, including the economic angles, and only mentions in any detail the project Höss and Wirths intended to launch in January 1944 with the support of the officer class. The project they'd been nurturing was the creation of a horseracing track in the Auschwitz Stammlager and stables for many more purebreds. Until then the camp had had few such horses, that is: four race horses, four for dressage, five for hunting and six pack horses. He wanted to emulate the great and renowned races that he used to see in Riem. Höss recommended his successor should continue flattening the ground in the area they had selected so no holes remained that might be lethal for horses' hoofs, and should delineate the boundaries of the race track with grave stones taken from Jewish cemeteries. Höss believed that the inhabitants of the two local cities, Auschwitz and Birkenau, as well as the soldiers garrisoned there, would come to the races, and that they would "sportingly" enliven camp life that was "overly mechanical and absorbed by the annihilation tasks we are carrying out." Obviously, there *is* another form of madness.

11

When the members of the *Sonderkommando* opened the gas chambers, the bodies were simply layers of limp flesh, with contorted rictus on every face, mouths gaping open and black tongues hanging out. It was a huge physical effort to extract the corpses from the pile one by one by pulling on an arm or a leg. Many children were locked tight in their mothers' arms and were impossible to separate out. They went into the ovens like that, mother and child together. If they were separated from their parents, they would be heaped together so they could be placed in a different oven ten at a time. That saved on space.

In order to move the bodies from the gas chamber to the adjacent ovens, they used ropes they put round necks in order to drag the bodies opposite the oven doors and then other men picked them up and threw them into the flames. The people responsible for pulling out gold teeth and cutting hair would often clamber into the gas chambers, trampling on corpses and climbing over the mountain of bodies that tended to form by the door, which those gassed had been desperately knocking on and screaming at. When they were on top of the human pile, they'd begin to push them down, make them roll over each other. The surface gave easily, there were lots of gaps and they often slipped and fell among the bodies and got mixed up with them. One of those men fell on the naked body of Sofia Pawlicka; he didn't know who she was—how could he?—but he did notice the astonishingly sweet composure on her face with its eyes closed, a trace of fleeting happiness, as if, at the moment of death, she had been courageous enough to remember something beautiful.

12

Rudolf Höss, the inventor of mass gassing techniques, ceased to be Auschwitz's chief commandant in December 1943 and became Chief Inspector of Department I in the Central Office for Concentration Camps, and was thus responsible for the supervision of all the extermination camps. His mission up to 1945 was to implement the liquidation programme established by Heydrich, Eichmann and Himmler. In the spring of 1944 he returned to Auschwitz in order to implement personally the elimination of 450,000 Hungarian Jews. The Third Reich, that according to Hitler's prophecy, was due to last a thousand years, capitulated in May, 1945. Summoned to the witness box, Höss proudly confessed, in a most matter-of-fact tone of voice, to the whole policy of extermination in the declaration he made at the Nuremberg trials. On March 11, 1947, two years after Hurbinek's death, Höss was judged in Warsaw and sentenced to death. He was hung on April 16 opposite Crematorium I in the Stammlager, on the exact spot where he had planned to put his racetrack.

X

ATTEMPTS TO RECLAIM A DREAM

1

In mid-April 1941, Sofia Cèrmik and Yakov Pawlicka went to Krakow on their honeymoon. They ignored the advice of parents and relatives, alarmed by the news coming from the city's ghetto, and fearful that, now that the whole of Poland belonged to the Reich, the invaders would prevent them from reaching their capricious destination, or even worse, would arrest and intern them in a camp, as it was rumored the SS was doing systematically. But Pavel Ramadian, Yakov's ingenious friend, provided them with forged papers, and a Mr. and Mrs. Jankowski booked into the Hotel Merkur on Krakowska Street. They lived on love, lived the unreality of newlyweds, distanced from fear, unaware that their dream was to shortly end in the most horrible of nightmares. When they left Rzeszów, waving their hands, more excited than they were happy, bidding farewell to friends and relatives, neither they nor anyone else present imagined that they would never return.

The Hotel Merkur was on the corner of the bustling, very commercial Józefa Street, which leads into the Kazimierz Jewish neighborhood, full of synagogues and small, shady gardens. But it is all abandoned now because the Jews have been forcefully enclosed within the southern ghetto, in Podgórze, a first step—although few know this as yet—to the extermination camp in Plaszów. Under their assumed names of Mr. and Mrs. Jankowski that aroused no suspicions on the part of the hotelier, a wary woman from the Carpathians, Sofia and Yakov rashly ignore the curfew in the ghetto, though it doesn't in fact affect them, since they are pretending not to be Jews, and they come and go throughout the city, convinced of their role as two young Poles in love, untouched by the occupation, and determinedly mundane, even frivolous, like dolls wrapped and boxed as a present for children who are starving to death.

I can picture Sofia. She is alone, leaning on the frame of their bedroom window. From her vantage point she can see the entrance to the ghetto, at the end of a long street. There, on both sides of the roadway furrowed by tramrails, are wooden barriers with a large number at the top indicating each door, and a sign in Gothic lettering, reminding the Jews that they face the death penalty if they leave that precinct. A car filled with German soldiers is parked on each side of the checkpoint. They look at papers and push and shove people.

I can see, or rather I should say that I imagine Sofia and her loneliness at four in the afternoon, waiting for Yakov to come back from an errand he is running for Samuel Pawlicka, his father. She is imagining everything she wants to do in these days of bliss, all that she associates with happiness and wants to happen. It is beyond her scope and she has to make choices. Thus, for example, she acknowledges that she is happy with the clothes she bought shortly after they arrived with the money her mother gave her—a red dress and shawl—in a shop recommended by Frankie, one of her cousins, who has now moved from Jakuba Street to the ghetto with Artur Sugar, her husband, and their daughters. Sofia and Yakov visited them on their first day in Krakow only to slope off, first repelled by the sad tedium of their visit with its meager offering of rancid Pomeranian jam, but driven above all by the desire to make love in their bedroom at the Merkur, making love conscious that they were different, new, untouched and pure compared with the filth in the lives of those living in the ghetto. They can neither believe it or reproach themselves. And then they will make love until they are blissfully consumed, at dawn, when, without their knowing, the ghetto doors open and many workers leave in trucks for the factories and some are shot down by bullets from drunken soldiers amusing themselves from the sidewalk, as the trucks drive by, with a little shooting range practice. But what can they know of any of that, if they are in the throes of love? Nausea and panic coexist parallel to their love. Anesthesia, consolation and self-defence are words Sofia once heard on the lips of her mother Raca's doctor, and stored away. Who could ever have anticipated she would use them now, in the midst of happiness.

But what is happiness? A pleasant, straightforward principle like a holy law: today happiness for Sofia is going out with Yakov to eat in a modest restaurant down the sidestreets of the old city, after walking down Grodzka Street, in Rynek Glowny, and then kissing passionately with wet lips under the century-old tower of the Town Hall. A German soldier on leave asked them to take a photo of him in the square with the tower in the background. Yakov took the camera and the German held Sofia by the arm, and she didn't resist. They both smiled as Yakov pressed the shutter release. Blissful ignorance of victims and their executioners. Now, I stiffen all of a sudden: what if that photo were the one I think my bedroom companion, here in Frankfurt, is using as a marker in the book he is reading? What if that photo were an old family photo, and that soldier—who never again saw that Polish couple, was unable to imagine they were two young Jews who barely two years hence were to enter a gas chamber, starving, humiliated, dying—were the father, uncle or grandfather of the man in the bed next to mine, who voted for the Social Democratic Party, is a Bayern Munich supporter and even has an extremely tolerant attitude toward Turkish immigrants, now that the Wall has fallen, and they are once again a single united Germany, a Germany *über alles*?

And what is happiness? I ask a second time. No doubt, for Sofia, it is about giving Yakov a hug in the fairground where they go every afternoon, before having dinner in a tavern that has Hungarian music, violins, tambourines and all that. They will get on the Ferris wheel they saw in the distance the day they arrived in the city and then go for a spin on the colorful carousel; she sits on his legs, while they whisper words of love and desire and she imagines herself back in bed at the Merkur under Yakov's embrace, intent, loving, gasping. Happiness for Sofia are those eternal moments when time comes to a halt, when she runs her fingers through Yakov's hair and nothing else matters; when night falls and together they don't feel the chill of Spring, despite the open window that looks over a gray street where paving stones have been lifted and brick walls plastered with orders from the Nazis, along which carts pass carrying corpses to the ghetto cemetery, where they beat youngsters who straggle behind, or perhaps say nothing and simply shoot them in the temples, *for the purposes of ethnic cleansing*. Neither Yakov nor Sofia are capable of understanding what is happening around them, in that street or in every street throughout the country, because love is deaf to gunshots; love is deaf to everything.

And is Sofia happy? Yes, she is, leaning on the window frame, watching the Nazis in their cars in the distance by the entrance to the ghetto, with a mind only for the imminent events of their evening that is about to begin: 1) Yakov will come—he's late, but he will soon be there— 2) they will leave the hotel, 3) he will cling to her waist and they will walk down the street, and 4) they will get on the Ferris wheel, their way to climb into the sky, and when they reach the very top, someone at the bottom will stop the motor for a few moments so they can survey the rooftops of Krakow and kiss. Fortunately for the pair of them, one cannot see the ghetto from the top of the Ferris wheel.

2

They were also together in Krakow just over a year ago, in February 1940. They told their families white lies, they said they'd be staying with cousin Frankie, though they stayed in a boarding house on Miodowa Street, in Kazimierz, with help from Frankie, who found them the best non-Jewish place in the neighborhood. On that occasion, the train journey was rather longer. Via an irony of fate, the train went through the city of Oświęcim without stopping. From their window they saw nothing odd on the outskirts of the town, except for large numbers of soldiers and howling dogs straining on their leashes everywhere. Himmler had yet to order the erection of the barbed wire fences, though the SS had arrived. Sofia was irrationally afraid for a few seconds, since she couldn't imagine the most crucial, intense moments in her short life would take place there, on that terrain the train was now leaving behind. A year later, on their honeymoon trip, everything in the area was slightly different: the train changed track before entering the town, with a points change in Babice. They saw men everywhere working under the eye of guards who were aiming their guns at them. Yakov assumed they had perhaps made a new branch line. There were still rails and crossties next to the soil dug up by the tracks. He told Sofia something amusing he had just remembered: Alfred Loewy, Kafka's uncle, had worked on that rail line in his youth as a second-grade administrator. Yakov knew that because he'd perhaps read about it in one of the Yiddish magazines in his parents' library. Yakov was a great admirer of Kafka.

"You see? We engineers also read," he then commented ironically to his wife.

On that occasion they spent four days and three nights in Krakow. The ghetto didn't exist as yet and the whole city had adapted to the hostile presence of the Wehrmacht and was returning to normal social life and entertainment, apparently unperturbed. Sofia and Yakov arrived in a city that was striving to get a feel for the artificial good cheer they all knew was threatened by brutal beatings, surprise round-ups and increasing murders of Jews in the streets and outskirts of Kazimierz. They all preferred to look the other way, unhappily, imperatively. The young couple loved to dance and, unworried as they were by the events slowly condemning the city, they simply looked for somewhere to let themselves go on the dance floor, something they could rarely or never do in Rzeszów, that was no more than a *shtetl* as far they were concerned. Consequently, when they saw a leaflet in their boarding house on Miodowa Street advertising a polka, mazurka and waltz competition, they didn't think twice about going along. It was on Bracka Street, in the old city, in a mansion that had been converted into a large café and dance hall, the Klub Camelot. It was packed with people pressed against each other and one could barely fit inside. The green of German uniforms predominated and cigarette smoke hung in a white pall over the heads of the dancers. An orchestra on a dais was playing a lively waltz and the couples eddying in the center of the floor made Sofia dizzy with excitement. She grabbed Yakov by the arm and kissed him on the cheek. She loved him and held her hands out toward him. They started to walk through the crowd. They quickly joined the whirlwind dancing and didn't stop the whole night. Waltzes gave way to polkas and polkas to the charleston, then back to a waltz, hour after hour. Sofia always danced with Yakov, but sometimes a young German soldier or another young Pole asked her for a dance. They all sweated and smelt of camphor or strong eau de cologne. The competition began at midnight and lasted for an hour, and the jury immediately started eliminating couples until they were down to three, one being Yakov and Sofia, who were awarded second place. When the owner of the dance hall handed them their prize he apologized, saying, "I'm sorry, there's no money for second prize, but you do get a voucher to come and dine here five nights for free."

Sofia and Yakov would leave the next day, as planned, so they couldn't enjoy their prize. That saddened Sofia but she perked up when she thought that Frankie and her husband Artur could certainly use the voucher. That made Sofia happy once again, and a few days later, when she was talking to her mother Raca, she kept repeating that the best part of the whole trip was being able to give that voucher to her cousin.

"I don't think they are very flush," she told her mother.

They returned to the boarding house in the early hours, occasionally dancing down the street and humming tunes the orchestra had played. The city was frozen and they saw no German soldiers on patrol. The disbelief prompted by being in that moment of history and that precise place meant Yakov and Sofia brimmed with contentment because life had given them the gift of knowing and loving each other. Nothing mattered apart from themselves. The world was a place where phantoms roamed amid the terror, but they alone were alive, and they alone had feelings. They hugged and kissed each other endlessly. Happiness dwelled up to the confines of their embracing bodies, and everything beyond was absurd, vapid and silly. It was the early morning of February 16, 1940 and that was the scene Sofia remembered on the final day of her life when they put her in a Birkenau gas chamber. She wanted to die remembering that now distant warmth from Yakov's body, but the other bodies, in that sealed chamber, were screaming too loudly in their despair.

3

Yakov has been delayed. He knows Sofia is waiting for him at the Merkur to go to the fair and the Ferris wheel. He has talked to her such a lot about that wheel! He couldn't have imagined it would take so long to find the bookshop owned by Simon Azvel, whom he owed a courtesy visit and news from his father, an old friend. He should have found the bookshop in an alleyway off Estery Street, but when he got there, after asking several questions that he phrased carefully depending on the appearance of the passers-by, he discovered the bookshop had in fact been bricked over and the number of the street scratched out with the point of a knife. Along the bottom someone had painted JUDE. He looked for another entrance via a front door and got access thanks to a concierge who peered out just then.

"Please, is Simon Azvel's bookshop here?"

"Of course, but Mr. Azvel has gone to live in Podgórze. He won't be back for a long time. Do you want a book? He left me in charge."

"No, I just wanted to give him my father's best wishes."

"I can easily open the shop. It's been bricked up outside by government order, as it is a Jew's business. You aren't Jewish, are you? I've got nothing against them but the law is there. They say they will all soon be forced to wear a white armband with the star of David, did you know that?"

"No, but I'm not Jewish," Yakov was quick to reply.

He said goodbye to the concierge, but before leaving had second thoughts and spoke to him again.

"Got any maps?"

"Yes, I think so."

"And postcards?"

"I couldn't say. Take a look for yourself. Come with me."

The concierge took a key from his pocket and opened a small door opposite his cubbyhole. He switched the light on. It was very dusty in the bookshop, but it didn't look untidy. Everything gave the impression they'd been forced to abandon it in a great hurry.

Yakov lingered looking for maps of Jamaica but didn't find any. On the other hand, he found a box with bundles of postcards tied round with a rubber band. Each bundle had a label with the country or region they were from. There were none from Jamaica, but nailed to the wall, above the place where the postcards were kept, was a 1931 calendar that said JAMAICA: VIEW OF KINGSTON HARBOR. It was a reproduction of an old English engraving of views of the bay where several sailing boats and steamers were anchored. Yakov interpreted this find as a piece of luck that was enough to justify his trip and frustrated visit to his father's friend. He insisted on buying it from the concierge but the concierge gave it to him as a present.

"I doubt Mr. Azvel will miss it, if he comes back," he said.

When he was back with Sofia in the Hotel Merkur, both of them lounged on the bed and stared at that old calendar for ages. Resting his head on Sofia's belly, Yakov daydreamed about going there one day; he told his wife it was the next best thing to Paradise and if they had children he couldn't think of a better place in the world for them to grow up than that island.

"It's better than Palestine. We'll have coffee plantations."

"But you don't even know if there is coffee in Jamaica," said Sofia.

"We will plant some," he said.

Then the noise of the boots of German soldiers on the sidewalk out in the street brought them back to reality. They were both suddenly scared and realized they were in danger. They held hands and their expressions clearly said that Jamaica didn't and couldn't exist. But the noise disappeared and was immediately forgotten. The loving couple went out to dinner before going on the Ferris wheel, as they had planned.

4

A few days later, Yakov and Sofia are strolling cheerfully through Krakow without a care in the world prompting knowing smiles from other passers-by. They walk along whispering very private, sometimes naively erotic sweet nothings to each other, most of them meaningless because they only show how love has put them in a world apart. They cross a bridge over the Vistula. The huge mass of Wawel Castle looms threateningly behind them.

They walk arm-in-arm, holding hands, feeling their faces almost cheek-to-cheek. Yakov is wearing a light-colored hat that doesn't match his dark striped suit. They innocently laugh and joke. Suddenly, a cyclist in sporting gear rides past at the end of the bridge and turns right before pedalling off at top speed. He seems to have broken away from the pack behind. Yakov loves cycling and watches him in awe like a wide-eyed child. The Pawlickas halt and watch the other cyclists race by and then realize it isn't a race but a single team, RKS Sport, the Polish champions, who are training on the outskirts of Wawel. Yakov applauds and cheers them on.

After skirting the rock under the fortress, the couple heads on to their destination for that morning, Poselska Street, and enters the Papugami Cinema. The film showing that day was *The Blue Angel*. Sofia thought the young Dietrich seemed frivolous and affected. Yakov found the stupid, cackling character of Professor Unrat very unpleasant, but maybe that was all to do with Emil Jannings, the actor playing Unrat, the Führer's favorite actor, together with Henny Porten, Zarah Leander and Jenny Jugo according to a magazine report he had read. A ghastly performance, Yakov decides. A young woman sold drinks during the intermission; Yakov wasn't to know this but he coincided at that drinks stall with Hans Haupt, the same Nazi officer who a few months later would lead off the convoy of trucks that was to take him and Sofia to Auschwitz in different vehicles. Shoulder to shoulder, now, in front of the refreshment seller, the two men don't look at each other, but they do collide slightly, quite unintentionally, before returning to ther seats. "I'm sorry," said Yakov. The officer said nothing and just politely waited for him to walk by.

5

On another occasion, a few days after their visit to the cinema, Yakov is wandering around the bookshops and antiquarians in the center searching unsuccessfully for maps of Jamaica like a hard-boiled collector. I picture him quite clearly, walking purposefully, seemingly at a loss, through the disturbing, suspicious city, hands in pockets, gabardine raincoat over one arm and hat on the tilt.

He goes in and out of bookshops, wastes time, and reclaims it thinking about the future, the big engineering enterprise he may set up in the city, while he waits for Sofia, whom he has agreed to meet in a couple of hours time, when she finishes her stroll down the shopping streets, on the trail of a present for him, a tie perhaps, cuff links or a handkerchief. While Yakov is poking around the street stalls, belonging to scared Jews, looking as if their minds were elsewhere, in another part of the city, Sofia stood outside the shop belonging to Josefina Luftig, who specializes in off-the-rack clothes for men (*prêt-a-porter*, as several signs next to the garments written in red ink indicate), where two dummies in the window wear suits and ties that she likes for her husband. Folded shirts, overcoats and jackets full of empty air hang on an invisible wire attached to the ceiling above the window display. Sofia finally walks in the shop and buys a pale purple shirt and a tie with a cheerful geometric pattern.

She remembers how on a previous occasion, in 1940, also on a trip with Yakov, she had entered that shop and bought nothing. She even remembers talking to Josefina Luftig, a slim woman, recently widowed, who was very jovial and animated and wore her hair tied back. Her children— she then told Sofia—worked with her in the shop. "We all make ends meet together," she concluded. Mrs. Luftig wasn't there now, and Sofia asked after her, prompted by no particular reason other than curiosity that was a prelude to fate, but no one could tell her where she was. Perhaps she was measuring up a customer in their house, the shop assistant suggested. She regretted not being able to say hello to her again. Nevertheless, Sofia did see Josefina Luftig again, but in the gas chamber, when they were both naked and, in an instinctive, desperate desire for a final gesture of affection, they embraced and died together.

6

The story of Mr. and Mrs. Jankowski was soon to come to an end. Two weeks after arriving in Krakow, Yakov and Sofia ran out of money and that killed off their fictitious, grand-sounding surname. They were back to being merely Mr. and Mrs. Pawlicka. They had to leave the Merkur Hotel on Krakowska Street and were welcomed in the ghetto by cousin Frankie's family. Life had started to become difficult for everyone, since, because of their race, they were unable to return to Rzeszów or leave the city. When someone in a restaurant identified them as Jews, they had had to leave their table and present themselves to the police in the street, who told them they were lucky because they'd already done in several Jewish pigs that morning ("Each got three bullets," grunted or laughed one of the policemen) and didn't feel like expending anymore sweat. They would simply leave them at the entrance to the ghetto, which is what they did, while on the way they several times tried to take off Sofia's clothes to a chorus of obscenities. "On other occasion they'd simply have shot you between your tits," cousin Frankie, not one to beat about the bush, later commented.

Initially their life in the ghetto wasn't so different from the life they'd been leading up to then in Krakow, even in a house in the worst possible state, lacking space, running water and light, because they were granted certain privileges as newlyweds. That meant they didn't have to contribute to daily domestic life, whether with money, of which they had none, or by helping with the most minor domestic chores. They even roamed the streets of Podgórze as if they were still on holiday. Although in that they were only imitating the vast majority of the ghetto's inhabitants, who packed the streets, huddled in tight little groups, and walked along with no particular purpose. Several times on their daily wanderings they met brother-in-law Artur and his daughters trying to find something to eat, sometimes even stealing food, as he would finally confess. Sofia and Yakov breathed a different kind of air: they made love when they went to bed and got up. After a frugal breakfast, they walked the streets casually trying to sell Frankie's family's candelabra though with no success. On the other hand, Sofia got into debt buying on a whim a stringbag for hats that she didn't need, and even Yakov borrowed money to buy cocoa sweets (from Jamaica, according to the wrapper!) that were on sale by a doorway where one night three violinists played a selection of the gloomiest music they could ever remember to a most miserable audience. That night Sofia longed for the cheerful waltzes and polkas in the Klub Camelot on Bracka Street that had intoxicated her a year ago as if she'd entered a new paradise. That word "paradise" was never to come to her lips again after listening to those searingly sad violins.

From then on, Sofia became aware of the relentless passage of time. Within a few weeks she realized people lumbering up and down the same street in a state of despair, and she kept bumping into the strangest of street hawkers: some sold orthopedic arms; others, potties; others, spools of colored thread; others, fishing rods; others, half-filled packets of cigarettes, pocket watches that had stopped, rusty knives, foil bracelets, turnips, and different sizes of stale bread. Others even set up a stall with magazines emblazoned with the effigy of Hitler and heroic scenes of the glorious German army in action.

Soon after, Sofia's eyes saw a growing number of beggars and every day more and more poor people who no one could help huddled on street corners. As the weeks passed by, starved corpses began to appear on the sidewalks.

One morning in July Sofia began to see dead children being strewn out on the streets. They looked like recently hunted animals. That same day she realized she'd been three months in the ghetto and was pregnant.

Then Sofia remembered something else. She recalled how in 1940, on their previous visit to the city, she and Yakov had visited the zoo, though they never actually went in, because a strange incident headed them off. Trumpet music was blasting next to a few fairground caravans and a man disguised from head to toe as a bear stood by the zoo fence. It was an ugly, much mended disguise. He was advertising a drink, as they gathered from the large poster by the fence next to the pile of the man's clothes. He was a gypsy, Yakov observed when the man removed his bear's head and passed round a tray for small change for the pirouettes and roars he'd been performing. When he was level with Sofia, he stared at her and clasped one of her hands between his fake bear paws, whose touch made Sofia feel slightly nauseous. "Get off your high horse, little princess, your children will end up like me," he told her. Then the man funneled his head back into the bear's and continued gesturing ferociously and frightening passers-by, until, another man, another gypsy, disguised as a hunter, rushed upon the scene from nowhere and started shooting the bear. After whimpering in a dying vein, he collapsed at Sofia's feet. The salvoes from the fake hunter scared away the zebras and gnus, and the condors in an adjacent cage flew off and crashed against the roof bars as did the pelicans and red-backed hawks. Wolves prowled around their sandy precinct and a climate of unnerving violence was suddenly unleashed in the zoo by the fence where the man disguised as a bear lay motionless on the ground. His colleague, who had acted the part of a hunter, saw his friend was taking far too long to get back on his feet and removed his bear's head. The gypsy had died from a heart attack. All that made a vivid impression on Sofia, who refused to go into the zoo and, very edgy, forced Yakov to accompany her back to their Miodowa Street boarding house. Alone in the ghetto, Sofia now remembered that event and that strange prophecy about her offspring and didn't know why but something terrible within her still led her to be afraid of her pregnancy, and she again became intensely aware of time and the little life she had left, as if she'd suddenly had an intuition that she would die young and would die soon: "Get off your high horse, little princess," the words uttered by that enigmatic man echoed round her head. And soon after, her dreams were rent with horror, "Abort . . . the Nazis will devour it . . . " or "He will never get out of the ghetto alive . . . " words the man disguised as a bear said in the middle of a nightmare she had every night for a week. She decided right away to speak to her cousin Frankie and find out where, and how, and how much money it would cost her to prevent that baby, *their* baby, from being born. That's why she said nothing to Yakov, because first she had to speak to Frankie, then act, take a decision and avoid adding more problems to the ones she already had. And all by herself.

8

In 1973 Federico Silla Accati made a present to his dear friend and partner Primo Levi of a book in Yiddish that had some chapters in Polish. It was a huge tome on chemistry in a fairly bad state of repair, with damp and mildew stains, missing its presumably colored illustrations. Its cardboard covers were battered at the corners. It was an elementary chemistry textbook, that bore no author's name, and simply said on the front *Chemistry Lessons. Publisher Yoel Huppert. Krakow 1937.* Accati had bought it by chance from a stall in the Jewish quarter of Turin. The fact it was written in Yiddish caught his attention, although he was even more surprised when he read inside, carefully written in Chinese ink, "This book belonged to Artur Sugar, Podgórze ghetto, 1941." Primo Levi thanked him for the present, was very moved, and thought it would be a way to keep the memory alive of at least one inhabitant of that ghetto that it was later discovered was entirely eliminated between the Plaszów and Auschwitz camps. But he could never have imagined that that copy was sold by Yakov Pawlicka, Hurbinek's father who never knew he was Hurbinek's father, on a July day in 1941, when he went into the only bookshop in the ghetto, sold his cousin Artur's book, asked if they had any books or postcards from Jamaica and if by chance they knew bookseller Simon Azvel. They had no books about Jamaica, and as for Azvel, he had been shot in the head in the ghetto and died.

9

How far away were her mother and her home! thought Sofia as she tortured herself with doubts about the life beginning to grow inside her. Because she wanted to have that child, wanted it more than anything else in the world.

And yet over a few months her hopes had given way to the brutal reality that had trapped her and made her feel painfully defenceless, far from her mother Raca's loving affections.

The scenes she saw daily in the streets of the ghetto were a perfect enactment of her fear and sense of living on the precipice. That couldn't be the life she would give her son. And then there were the lists prepared by the Jewish police, who hunted out people for the SS and sent entire families to the camp in Plaszów. What happened to them there? Sofia wondered. Had any member of any family ever returned to tell their story? What newly born child could survive the conditions in a camp? But Sofia couldn't imagine how removed from reality were the scenes going through her mind, because she had next to no idea, when she tried to think through her fears, of what a real concentration camp was like. No, she wouldn't have her child, she convinced herself, then immediately changed her mind: yes, yes, she would have it. Frankie her cousin never found out because Sofia never got to ask her advice and ask her to help her abort.

Over the course of those days, she avoided Yakov, who was forced to sell his calendar with views of Jamaica and was very grief-stricken. Unable to hide her sorrow sufficiently not to arouse suspicions, she tried to ensure people didn't see her looking so worried. She finally asked Frankie to send her apologies to Yakov and Artur because she was suffering from "women's things." That sparked off in Yakov intense, cheerful curiosity just in case those "women's things" were a euphemism for pregnancy, which Sofia categorically denied. But Yakov's ingenuous glee encouraged her to think yes, she would have that child, whatever the cost. Let life run its course, she finally decided to her relief, though she still tormented herself by thinking how immensely stupid she had been to get pregnant in that place at that time. She reproached herself for such an irresponsible blunder.

And all because she couldn't stand the way life was so precarious. It annoyed her, although she knew she couldn't do anything about it: their executioners wanted to starve them to death and were succeeding since everything was so scarce. Clothes, for example, soon wore thin and had to be patched and re-patched. Shoes, for example, broke and there was no way to get new ones. She saw so many people walking barefoot down the streets, or people who had created shoes out of strips of felt or jute! But felt and jute were also in short supply! And then there was the filth. And illness. And petty hates: people argued, came to blows, even wrought revenge and killed their own neighbors, tired of having to share every inch of ground and every minute of life in the ghetto.

Then Sofia and Yakov suffered their worst ever experience in the time they'd been there. One afternoon, when they were walking along, silently, aimlessly, they came to the cemetery; they went a few feet inside from the street and saw how carts kept coming in piled high with bodies without coffins. They saw how frightened, tearful adolescents put them in barrows that were destined for open graves splattered with quicklime. That was the moment when Jamaica ceased to exist for Yakov and the memories of Rzeszów and their happy moments, laughter, caresses and security in the family house, and their favorite smells and tastes ceased to exist for both of them. Everything sank deep into that enormous open grave they could see from the entrance to the cemetery. Goodbye as well to the future, to plans for an engineering business, or plans to study the engines of tanks, tractors, Mercedes Benz and BMW. Goodbye to any possibility. Time was no longer moving forward; time had ground to a halt.

"Now we'll never grow old," said Sofia, giving Yakov a hug and looking away from the grave.

"It makes no sense to talk about the future," said Yakov grimly while he stroked Sofia's hair.

"Yakov, all our future now is what happens tomorrow, and I can't much believe in tomorrow," said Sofia.

"My love, I so miss the time when we were children in Rzeszów and no one was persecuting us," said Yakov.

They stayed silent, united in their embrace, while nearby the burial people continued their sad round of work. Yakov suddenly separated out from Sofia, looked her in the eyes and said, "I am glad you aren't pregnant. I don't want us to have children. Promise me we will never have children, promise!"

"I promise," replied Sofia without hesitating. She'd decided to abort. Yakov was right. The very different words Yakov had said to her on their wedding day rushed into her head, "We will have lots of children and I will love you for a hundred years." Reality changes everything.

10

Chaos came on August 7.

The morning when Sofia had decided to tell Yakov the truth about her pregnancy and the decision she'd finally taken, he left the house very early with Artur. Sofia got up feeling sick and saw cousin Frankie in the kitchen. She didn't feel spirited enough to ask her right then whether she knew anyone who carried out abortions. A forlorn tension haunted her eyes, and she avoided her cousin's gaze so as not to betray her thoughts. Instead, Frankie, who was in a good mood, rattled on and on about Artur having to get up earlier and earlier in order to try and sell the books from his chemistry teacher's library, and how he'd discovered he could make more money if he sold them separately but he had to get up earlier, almost when it was still nighttime, to find a buyer, because everything was now being bought and sold in the ghetto. Then she spoke about a dress she'd have to sell sooner or later. Sofia's worries were thus buried beneath a pile of trivia and she gradually relaxed.

At eight o'clock they heard brakes screeching down in the street, followed by loud shouting. Sofia looked out of the window and saw lots of soldiers running in every direction, including toward the entrance to their house. The sound of boots got louder and louder. Shots were suddenly being fired on the staircase. They banged on their door. Frankie's daughters woke up frightened and Sofia and her cousin looked at each other. They said things, perhaps the most important sentences they'd ever uttered, but didn't hear each other. They banged insistently on the door. Once, twice. The third time, Frankie, shaking all over, walked over to open the door, but a burst of submachine gunfire from the stairs hit her in the chest and she crashed to the floor. Four bleeding wounds streaked her front from her shoulders to her pelvis. She was lying on her back, her eyes open. Sofia, panic-stricken, couldn't think what to do. However, pushed and shoved by the soldier responsible for the shooting she had the presence of mind to shield the daughters from the sight of their mother's corpse as they left the flat. It had all happened very quickly. Two or three minutes.

In the street they were separating men from women and forcing them into trucks. Sofia walked as if through the air, dragged along by the inertia of hundreds of women who, screaming and panicking, were being pulled, like her, this way and that by the different huddles around the trucks. In one of these to-ings and fro-ings she lost the girls, who were put in another truck. She was left feeling desperate. Was *that* really happening?

She couldn't bring any order to the thoughts in her head. She reacted quickly, but her brain went thick and fuzzy as she had to struggle not to fall to the ground, because they shot or rifle-butted to death anyone who fell down. She gradually became aware of the extent of the horror she was facing. In the wake of her cousin's death, the mere thought of which made her shake in fear, she now realized she would never see Yakov again, or Artur, or the girls, that Yakov would never find her, and that idea distressed her more than any other. She started to imagine, with all the sorrow her soul held, that Yakov was already dead, that he might have been one who fell trying to escape or running off thinking he had a chance, because Yakov always thought he had a chance and was always sure of himself. Those are the brave ones. Then, when she was being shoved into a truck, she thought she spotted Yakov and Artur in another truck.

"Yakov! Yakov! Yakov!" she shouted from the truck she managed to peer out of after she'd pushed three women away with her fists, but her voice was inaudible above the screams and wailing.

Then she lost sight of the truck where she thought she'd seen Yakov and Artur. It had left with the convoy of men. It was an illusion, a mirage of Sofia's. Yet it was true: Yakov and Artur were in that truck, were on their way to Auschwitz where Artur would be gassed on arrival. They had been arrested two blocks from their house, still carrying the book they were hoping to sell. Yakov didn't see Sofia's truck, but he was certain they'd only rounded up men that day, that the women were safe. Artur, on the other hand, was more pessimistic. He knew that they'd already emptied several blocks of dwellings so they could demolish them later on. If not, where did those empty lots in the ghetto suddenly appear from? It was like eliminating animal burrows.

How quickly happiness had disappeared! thought Sofia, devastated in the back of the truck that hadn't driven off, that was parked in the street, still as an island of grief: you only had to see the faces of the women and girls huddled next to her. Only she and her unborn son existed at the end of that tunnel that the small universe of her life had entered that morning. Sofia now saw it clearly—the child, who in her plans, despite herself, ought to die, would perhaps be the only one of them to survive. In some paradoxically cruel way the Germans had decided for her: they wanted him for themselves, fate was taking possession of that child.

Sofia stopped talking to her son as if he were someone who'd never exist, someone dead in her belly, and now began to beg he'd have what she most liked about Yakov, his good sense of humor, cheerfulness, sweet charm, nobility, innocence and courage. She wanted her son to inherit all that from his father whom she was sure he would never meet. Her firm desire to give birth to that child now gave new value to her existence. She didn't know where she was heading, but her son would be born.

At eleven thirty, the truck that took Sofia to the camp in Auschwitz finally drove off.

XI

OUR BODIES ARE ALL THAT WE HAVE

1

Born on the snow.

On March 5, 1942, at 8:55 a.m., Sofia Pawlicka, Cèrmik by her maiden name, from Rzeszów, went into labor and gave birth to a boy in a hidden corner of barrack 115 in the women's camp in Birkenau, in Auschwitz II. It was snowing and the temperature had gone down to several degrees below zero. The baby was small and scrawny because his mother was so weak and everything suggested he wouldn't survive.

Sofia had to endure many afflictions, especially to avoid her pregnancy being noticed during roll call and conceal the changes her body, that grew from month to month, was undergoing. Other women prisoners told her what happened to pregnant women when they reached Auschwitz, and she was determined that wouldn't happen to her as long as she was alive and she would draw on all her strength to hide that son she carried within her from the Germans. And she succeeded in keeping it secret for several months. To that end, she stayed still, almost paralyzed for long periods of time in places the female SS didn't usually search, like underneath the barrack, where the prisoners had made a hole for her, where she crouched for hours until she couldn't feel her legs, that were stiff and numb, or fainted from nervous stress. She also hid inside the latrines or underneath the bunks, right up against the wall, on her back in a space where she could hardly breathe, where rats and insects passed constantly.

In fact most of the pregnant women Sofia heard about were taken to a barrack set apart for them, V3 in Birkenau, three hundred feet or so from barrack 115. They generally kept some seventy or eighty desperate women in there, who arrived with the faint maternal hope they could save their children, but immediately went mad when they discovered what the real purpose of that barrack was. However, nobody lasted long in that place. They provoked premature, aborted births through injections of chemicals or via blows or kicks delivered by the female camp guards. In both cases, mother and child sometimes died simultaneously. I have often wondered why they didn't gas them straight away when they got off the trains or trucks. But they didn't because the arbitrary mentality of the Nazis acted in formal, mechanical ways when it came to setting up procedures, and a pregnancy was just another procedure, naturally to produce a life that would have to be immediately terminated, but nevertheless it had to follow its own procedure, except in those cases when a mother resisted too fiercely when being led to the labor barrack, and then she would be sent straight to the gas chambers without a moment's hesitation. If they didn't abort and did finally give birth, the SS women snatched the babies from their mother's arms and killed them immediately, sometimes in the mothers' presence, by submerging their heads in buckets of water. There were cases when they were handed over to be sent to Germany to be subjected to a programme of *Aryanization*—if the child was fair-haired and blue-eyed. The mothers never knew what the fate of their children was and, generally, soon died from septicemia, since they were taken to the filthiest of barracks where they bled to death or contracted lethal diseases.

Sofia gave birth in the spot under the barrack where she had hidden so often. Crouching, she gave birth on the snow, silently, clenching her lips so she didn't scream, helped by Sara Ruda Malach—a fellow prisoner and mother of three children that died in the ghetto—who severed her umbilical cord with her teeth. Then they carefully wrapped the child in rags and hid him between straw mattresses. They ran the risk that his crying might betray everyone in the barrack, that they might all be gassed for concealing that child. They were even afraid he would choke to death because Sofia was so rigorous in her efforts to hide him from the female guards. Moreover, Sofia and some of the other prisoners who were aware of the baby's existence knew there were real dangers they could only fend off with prayers: they knew she could barely feed her child, for whom there was no medicine, that it was freezing cold and that there were the loathsome rats that were Sofia's obsession ever since the day she saw, near where she was hiding under the barrack, rats fighting and biting over an abandoned baby next to its dead mother. But then a time came when she was forced to think, even if only to herself, against her feelings of tenderness, that that protection was simply a slow death sentence, that sooner or later they would find him, they would find her baby. To proclaim his existence would amount to executing him herself; hoping for a miracle was futile. And she couldn't cry, her tears had dried up forever. But she would let life decide rather than surrender. And she began by giving him a name: Ari. Yakov would have liked that name. That name and body that were now breathing together in spite of everything.

"You are Ari. Your name is Ari. I hope you'll be able to say it some day," Sofia told the child she pressed against her breast, in a faint murmur fraught with silence. The camp's snow-covered esplanade was beginning to awaken to the realization of hard facts invading like nightmares.

So then, Hurbinek was really Ari. Ari Pawlicka, at least once and only from the whispering lips of his mother. Primo Levi never knew. Henek didn't either. No one ever did.

2

The closeness of bodies.

When I was in Moscow in 1989 I saw a woman who looked as I imagined the mother of Hurbinek—really Ari—to be, that Hurbinek I am creating as Sofia created hers. She was small and vivacious, beautiful and firm, but looked ill. She walked slowly and her glance was very expressive. We were very close for a moment. Then she went on her way without noticing me. Her face stayed with me. I don't really know why. When I was thinking about Sofia, here, in my room in a Frankfurt hospital, I suddenly thought of that woman I had walked past in the GUM Department Stores and realized that the moment had come to give that memory substance. It was a face from the future I encountered in the past to illustrate a much greater past I entered as an intruder. She had Sofia's sweet, slightly pale, emaciated face, with prominent bags under eyes that depressed her eye sockets even deeper, perhaps as a result of poor food, or a complete lack of food, or an illness, tuberculosis perhaps. That spectral, skinny face that had suddenly aged, is how I imagine Sofia's to be, in the weeks after she gave birth.

In barrack 115, packed with bodies that now have nothing, that are themselves their only possession and only identity, Sofia is nursing Ari, always in a state of terrified alert. But she doesn't eat. Only now and then her Hungarian friend, Sara Ruda Malach, keeps back for her a ration of potato soup. "Our body is what we are, all we have," Sofia thinks, when she sees herself surrounded by other bodies, bodies everywhere, whose ages no one could ever guess: elderly girls, elderly women bereft of flesh and future, women surviving daily the selection that takes hundreds to the gas chamber. Bodies close to each other. "The immeasurability of immediate closeness," Walter Benjamin wrote somewhere, as I now recall. How can one measure one's own history, that brims over in contact with another body, when there is no privacy for bodies that are complete strangers, that don't love each other, that wouldn't even know of their existence if it weren't for that togetherness forced upon them by the camp, that absurd cruelty, reduction to zero, unavoidable reduction to a common fate?

Bodies, in Auschwitz, are near one another, and protect, abhor, detest, touch, accompany one another. Some bodies steal subtly from others (like, for example, the body that snatches from another dying body its bowl of soup, thus enacting life's implacable law); or snitch on other sick bodies so they take them away, they don't want to know where—although, of course, they know!—and leave space for those remaining, and leave blankets and shoes. But then the body that has snitched realizes the empty space is being filled by two or three additional bodies, that fight over that space, those shoes and that blanket. Bodies that will finally want to embrace any body whatsoever before dying, as Sofia will do in the last second of her life, several months later.

At night, among the bodies sleeping in barrack 115, Sofia left Ari in the straw and put a small, not very tight muzzle over his mouth to deaden the sound of his frequent, unexpected crying. She knew Ari might choke, but Sofia preferred that terrible possibility to the certainty he would be murdered if his existence were discovered. On many such nights when she couldn't get to sleep, as in the many preceding months, she tortured herself repeatedly thinking about how she didn't know what had happened to Yakov. She didn't want to think he was dead, though she took it for granted on days she felt particularly pessimistic. At other moments she would let herself be lulled by a timid hope, and thought how he must be well and out of that camp; then she'd be tortured by the sorrow Yakov would feel when he thought of her and searched for her everywhere, futilely, never finding her, as he never found Azvel the old bookseller, and never found any views of Jamaica. But Sofia could never know when she was thinking of her family, for example, that they were really so close. Her father-in-law Samuel Pawlicka and her brother-in-law David died in Auschwitz, a few barracks away, days after Ari was born, that March 5, and worst of all, her elder brothers, Aaron and Stefan Cèrmik, taken in a round-up in Rzeszów and hurled into a cattle truck that dropped them on a platform in Auschwitz at midnight, were gassed at the very moment she arrived in the camp. The bodies, beloved bodies of beloved beings, had for a time been close, very close, gathered together forever.

But later when Ari was two months old, he began to be her greatest torture. And the torture grew because only she knew when she had those unexpected flashes of that horrific though righteous thought about killing him with her own hands, to save him from all that future pain. A thought that came to her the first time under barrack 115, immediately after her son was born. She'd never ruled it out completely. It was her most private, lacerating secret. Then, she thought, if she did do it, she'd throw herself at the electrified fence. She wouldn't be able to live a second more.

She was tortured by the filth in which they lived, a source of infection for Ari and herself. What would be of her son if she died first? The clothing wrapped around Ari was full of bits from his defecations, earth and grease stains, bits of other people's dirt, filth that carried the filth of others. And yet Sofia had got over her revulsion. One day she discovered her own body had sores. She'd been infected with horrible boils, her friend Sara Ruda was to blame, devored as she was by lice and fleas, and the boy as well. The sores had reached her mouth, that was covered in ulcers, just like her baby's, whose lips were strips of raw flesh. Moreover, Ari wasn't growing; he fitted in the small hollow shaped by her hands.

Time went by, Ari was three months old. Feeding him was agony as death drew nearer and nearer. A prisoner, who said she was a doctor, although she'd admitted to Sofia she had in fact only been a doctor's lover, confirmed that malnutrition was advancing. Sofia could do nothing; she was one more defeated woman.

The evasive glances from the other bodies refused to meet hers. They were forlorn glances. And I imagine and see them in Frankfurt, exchanged by the patients in this hospital, as I've seen them at other times in my life. It is easy enough, if you know how. They meld with uneasy looks: what's happening, what's dream, what's reality. And the glances finally become disconsolable grief. They watched Sofia in her colossal struggle to keep her child alive, but they knew that today or tomorrow neither would be there. Dream: no dreams were possible, only a dream of eating. Dreams cannot be interpreted, cannot be deciphered in terms of any another reality. Dreams are what they are, an additional, different, distanced reality. Sofia would like to dream of food, of food for her and her son. But she avoided dreams, avoided that luxury, even avoided sleep, because when she slept, exhausted by tiredness, Sofia knew that when she woke up, Ari's body, in her lap, an extension of herself, might perhaps be frozen or crushed.

No one laughs.
My thoughts now turned back to Yakov. He arrived
in the camp the same week as Sofia, after spending
several days exposed to the elements in Plaszów,
where an SS officer put an unloaded revolver to his
temple every morning, laughed and said, "Tomorrow,
tomorrow, right!" He came in a truck that formed
part of a convoy of twenty-two trucks packed with
Jews from the whole of Galicia. He recognized faces
from the Podgórze ghetto and was scared. He was still
with Artur, who kept by his side all the time, weeping
despondently, interminably, when he thought of his
daughters and Frankie, whose murder was unknown
to him. But Artur was separated from him as soon as
they reached Auschwitz, and taken with the majority of
those men to the barrack next to the gas chambers and
crematoria. Yakov said goodbye because he knew where
his friend was headed.

They sent the remainder to a large esplanade before
allotting them to a barrack. They forced them to witness
one of the frequent executions. It was an old man and a
young man, barely an adolescent. They were on the point
of hanging them, had just put a rope round their necks.
The scaffold was very basic, made from white timber; it
rocked at every movement; prisoners were underneath
with barrows ready to collect the bodies. Only the fifteen-
year-old whimpered things Yakov, who happened to be in
the front row, couldn't understand. He was Russian and
had pushed a German soldier who was whipping the old

man. Now both young man and old were paying for that with a lesson for everyone.

Later on, in the barrack, Yakov's thoughts returned to those he had left behind. To his family in Rzeszów, to his beloved Sofia, who he thought was free along with Frankie somewhere in the ghetto or perhaps, in his most utopian moments, had escaped from there and been hidden by Raca in a corner of her big house on Targova Street. His imagination couldn't harbor anything tainted by reality. He didn't know the fates of his father and brother. He didn't know Sofia was pregnant. After a few months, Yakov would wander through the camp, would go to and from the Krupp workshops where he worked as a slave, and not even suspect that his own son, whose existence he was totally unaware of, would be born and survive in that appalling factory of death.

Meanwhile Yakov had seen other men go into decline, robust men, people with faith, true fighters. They were transformed into the living dead, and then hunted down and *selected*. He knows the ability to resist has its limits and keeps repeating that to himself. But those limits are extensive; he is still one resisting inside that kind of filthy rabbit farm, he thought, destined to be fodder for the slaughterhouse or mere skins. They resisted beyond all manner of belief. That was supreme courage, success at survival. He was thinking about resistance the day Ari was born, about strength taken from where there no longer was anymore. If he went to sleep thinking along those same lines, it was because he had entered a strange twilight zone, a mental place where he located himself to see what he would become the day after. He saw himself as if he were someone else, stronger and not in retreat.

One day he laughed. He was looking after another seriously ill prisoner who was so skinny he seemed to float in the air. The man would die the day after. In the midst of that wretchedness, the sickly man burst out laughing as if he were coughing, and took from his pocket a soft, wrinkled potato on which someone had etched a caricature of Hitler. He handed it to Yakov who burst out laughing; he wasn't sure why, perhaps it was the potato's ridiculous shape or the grotesqueness of the situation. However, he went on laughing and Yakov had to put one hand over the sick man's mouth as he placed the other over his own. The man convulsed and was soon back in his moribund state. Yakov shamelessly devoured the potato there and then. That night, appalled once again by that affliction but astonished to be still alive, Yakov realized he missed laughter, or rather, when he thought of that afternoon's occurrence, he remembered that sensation actually did exist though he'd quite forgotten what it was like. Laughter didn't emerge, not even in the case of those who went crazy. There were no laughs. No one laughed in the camp, except for the guards when they were doing their work in a good mood.

4

Fear in the blood.

Maria Mandel was a tall, lean woman, who always looked rage-stricken, with her hair tied back and an unpleasant expression on her lips, as if in a continual mix of repulsion and ironic smile. A photo exists of her saluting Himmler when he visited the camp. She is next to Wirths. Whenever she spoke, she screamed piercingly and displayed her uneven teeth. She was Head of the Women's Camp and was known as *The Beast* because of her extreme brutality. Others called her *The Spider*, because of the way she wove her webs to catch the prisoners' hidden children. That was her mission in life and she applied herself with exaggerated zeal. She had received her training in the Ravensbrück camp, where she left in her wake a reputation as a merciless murderer. She was always preceded by two female SS. She would tour the barracks daily and walk in without prior warning, acting like a hunter mounting an ambush. The prisoners shook when they saw her come in because they never knew what to expect. What *The Beast* thought was right one day was wrong the next, what was recommended one day was forbidden the next: a piece of cloth like a scarf on someone's head annoyed her one day (and she was capable of killing the individual involved just for that) and the day after, on the contrary, she'd linger tying a knot in a morbid maternal spirit on the head of a pale, motionless prisoner.

Any sideways glance that met with hers was a challenge that called for humiliation. She would react, beside herself, furiously punching and kicking her victim in the belly. They found it hard to separate her out from the victim she would beat with gloved hands or a chain she wore round her waist. When she finished the job, she was so red in the face and sweating so much, that the SS had to prise her off and prop her up, she was so exhausted. In 1947, when she was sentenced to death and they were about to hang her, someone at the foot of the scaffold reminded her how she had killed eight hundred women with her own hands. She bawled for one last time, flashing the whites of her eyes, in an indication it wasn't very many.

Sofia had seen her several times and suffered one of her attacks in June 1942. *The Beast* had walked into barrack 115 in the middle of the morning; at the time Sofia was looking after Ari, but couldn't react quickly enough to hide him. When the two SS women ordered them imperiously to stand in a row, she only had time to put the gag in her baby's mouth and hand him over to Sara Ruda who hid under the wooden bunks during the entire visit of *Frau* Mandel. To help Sara, Sofia distracted the brutal woman by mentioning that there was no wood or coal left for the stove. Without saying a word, Maria Mandel let go a slap that made her collapse on the ground. She undid her chain, started bawling and hitting her remorselessly.

"You fool! There are no stoves for you in summer, you shitty Jew, there are no stoves for you!" she shouted in the foulest of tempers.

Sofia protected herself as best she could, but too many blows were raining down. Why so much punishment for such a trifle, she wondered. She passed out, she was so weak. The worst about that visit wasn't the savage beating she received, but the fear she was left with, terrible fear in her body because she had brought herself to the attention of *Frau* Mandel and sensed she would be back, that she wouldn't leave her in peace and in the end would discover Ari.

She imagined this and her blood froze when another woman appeared in her mind, who, like her, was hiding her small child in the barrack's hellish nooks and crannies. Her name was Barbara Breonka and she was Czech.

They had caught her making a kind of pap from the daily broth and dry black bread, to which she'd added a small piece of potato. She was crumbling it with her fingers to make it softer. The Mandel woman spotted her and was suspicious. There were lots in her position; she had already rooted out more than forty and in every case both mother and child had died, but only after being tortured.

When *Frau* Mandel took hold of the baby Barbara Breonka had tied to her lap and that was beginning to wriggle free, she ordered all the women in the neighboring barracks to line up opposite the barbed wire fences. She placed the woman in front of them and the child on the ground. She took the baby's clothes off. It wasn't yet six month's old, was tiny and was crying. *The Beast* then crossed her arms and waited silently for one of the women who couldn't stand it any longer to clutch at the baby in order to pick it up off the ground. *Frau* Mandel suddenly burst into song. Sofia recognized the music she'd heard on her parents' gramophone.

It was a cruel torture for Sofia to see that child turn purple and move on the ground that cold morning. She scratched her wrists in anguish. An old woman ran to help the baby, knowing it was a suicidal act, and was cut down by a bullet from one of the watch towers.

"Bravo, you good Jew!" *Frau* Mandel exclaimed. And started singing again.

The dead woman thus lost all she had, all she was, she lost her body, thought Sofia while her eyes tried to avoid that bundle stretched on the ground, and her mind went off to distant beech woods and meadows they couldn't see, as eternal as the vineyards and cherry and chestnut trees on the hills of Rzeszów. That old woman no longer existed. All the other women were horrified. After standing in front of that cruel spectacle for a few hours, Frau Mandel gave out orders for the mother to be taken to the gas chambers and for the rest to go back to their barracks. The baby was left there, and there it died in the afternoon.

5

Saying goodbye forever.

She heard the trains arriving when she couldn't get to sleep in the barrack; she identified the whistle of that train; it was like the one that took her and Yakov to Krakow when they were so much in love; she identified the whistles, the sound of the engine; she was also familiar with the howls of the dogs and wondered about Yakov. Might he be in one of those? How could she look for her husband? She was in despair because she was sure he was there, in the camp, somewhere. But then she began to think more coldly and was consoled by the macabre hope that he might be dead, she told herself, all his suffering must be at an end. But there are no more beautiful funerals. Death in Auschwitz was wretched and extremely mechanical, a routine that neither angered nor shocked anyone.

Thinking those thoughts, in November 1942, four months before she died, Sofia decided to separate out from her son. *Frau* Mandel was sniffing avidly around and she couldn't continue to play with his fate. The danger was immense and a possible scenario of Ari in *The Beast's* hands horrified her. The checks, when they only found wretchedness and the odd corpse that nobody had noticed—perhaps because the person seemed to be asleep—became more frequent, and *Frau* Mandel's interrogations more aggressive and cruel. Now that her dear friend and accomplice, Sara Ruda, had died at the end of summer, she was afraid the rest of the women wouldn't tolerate Ari and would betray him. Yes, she must separate out from Ari, she must not think about herself but the fact that he could be saved. Whatever the cost.

Sofia began to harbor vague hopes when she heard rumors that there had been cases of babies born in the camp who'd been successfully smuggled out and taken to places unknown. Ada Neufeld had told her about that, Ada, one of the women who, like her, had been in the camp the longest. She also warned her she would possibly never see her son again. That was the price. Sofia accepted the price and paid with her sorrow. She needed to believe it was possible.

One cold night she left him, in the open, on the ground under the barrack's false floor, the same place where she had given birth. Before she went through the hole back into the barrack, she felt Ari's heart between his ribs. She touched his face lingeringly, as if she were trying to hold on to every inch of his skin, every fold and feature. She knew she would only be left with memories. He was very cold, it was winter and he was shivering. She breathed on his cheeks and hands; then pulled tight the tattered strips of blanket wrapped around him. She said goodbye with one last glance, sadly, disconsolately. She murmured "my little love" and went back inside.

She kept waiting, fighting the temptation to look and see if he was still there. Ada had told her. And she had risked it. Maybe the women were well organized, the plan would work out, there was someone trustworthy pulling the strings. They would pick him up, as had been agreed, when there was a change of guard. Sofia couldn't know who did it, whether a heroic prisoner or a guard who had felt remorse. Nor did she know how or when he would leave the camp, or where they would hide him from Mandel's violence. A feeling of guilt ran through her, her sorrow was unbearable for a few moments and she choked on her silent anguish. All that potential life she would no longer live with her son, a life as happy as the life she'd lived with her parents in Rzeszów, passed before her eyes and vanished. "Goodbye, goodbye," that life not lived with her son seemed to say. Dreams also say goodbye, she thought. She quickly opened the trapdoor at the back of the barrack and put her head out. Ari had gone.

Over the next four months Sofia regretted doing what she had done, and succumbed to the wracking uncertainty about what might have been her son's fate. She tried to find him, but Ada Neufeld, the only one who could give her a clue, was *selected* a few weeks after organising Ari's exit. Her regret morphed into a passive attitude in relation to her own fate. She had discovered the dialect of death, that was to do nothing to avoid it, to sink into quiet stagnation. Sick and starving, she dragged her feet and sat in the puddles on the camp, splashing rhythmically, totally in a void. It was the prelude to death and she let herself be swept away by an irresistible tide. She no longer even closed the eyes of those who died beside her. She felt scornful and hollow. She sighed for Yakov and hated herself for letting them snatch Ari from her. She only found consolation in the idea, entertained because it was so impossible, that she would be able to repeat her life, to start all over again. Though when she had such thoughts, she always reached the same conclusion: life is utterly treacherous and so inevitable.

6

Saved by madness.

Yakov, Yakov! It is the rainy month of May 1943. Sofia is dead and Yakov's teeth have started to fall out. His strength is now inhabited by the fragile remnant of a human being. He caught diphtheria and his gums are turning black. I feel great compassion for him as I imagine him in my bed in this Frankfurt hospital from which I will soon be discharged. He wanders senselessly, unaware of his son's existence, of his wife's death, a kind of unbalanced, frightened, skeletal character from Dante. He wanders senselessly, only responds to the fear that beats in every corner of the camp: when he hears the SS corporal utter the words "Jewish pig!" aimed at someone else, he automatically puts his arms over his face to shield himself against the coming blow.

The Yakov I imagine hears music in the air and stops and listens opposite the barrack entrance, in the middle of the main road. He tries to look up high to find out where it is coming from, to glimpse the secret to the delightful sound only he has heard. He looks toward the sky as if experiencing an epiphany. The guard is hitting his feet with his gun and Yakov howls and doesn't understand why the German is tittering and then says, "a bird will shit on you or lightning will strike you down, you imbecile!"

Yakov gradually lost his mind, in a few weeks. First came symptoms of disarray, he was bewildered doing the work he was forced to do in the Krupp factory where he'd been sent. What am I doing here? Is this Jamaica? he wondered uneasily and it took him a few minutes to understand the reality surrounding him. He looked in every direction and sometimes it seemed like a fairground, at others a castle, and others a slaughterhouse. He'd lost his sense of identity. He'd even lost any notion of death. He stacked weighty objects, they made him carry beams from one side to the other, following criteria that were completely arbitrary, as he would have to carry the same beams back to the spot where they'd been before. Or else bricks (and if he dropped one, they would rifle-butt him in the back and he'd collapse). Or else he'd be interminably unloading steel bars or barrels of oil off the backs of trucks. His hands often went numb and he frequently had to rub them together.

Later on, he'd suddenly start attacking the prisoner next to him, no matter who, and would punch and abuse him hysterically. No one understood why he acted in that hateful way, but it was futile to try to get him to understand how ridiculous he was being because they assumed he was striking out against the impotence they all felt.

A few days after he began to confuse objects and people and speak to himself or empty space. The guards mocked him, tripped him so he fell to the ground and insulted him.

"Talk to my helmet," they'd say as they laughed. The mad Jew entertained them. He thanked them and bowed to them, he'd lost his grip on reality and thought he was an actor on stage.

"I am happy, I am happy. Thank you, thank you," he kept repeating to the other bemused prisoners who had finally decided to ignore him.

In a short time he had become a buffoon whose death the guards had already assigned a date. What good was that idiot to them? By June he was completely mad: he imitated German with words that he made up, and that provoked the same hilarity in the guards as if they'd been in a comic cabaret in pre-war Berlin, and he'd bang his head against the walls of the barrack. Nobody saw to his injuries and they became infected. The day he was *selected* he gave out blessings left and right in a Latin he had heard in church. *Dominus vobiscum . . . Ora pro nobis . . . Amen, amen, amen . . .* He never understood what was happening and thought the gas chamber was the ocean liner that was finally going to take him to Jamaica. His last words were, "It's about to set sail." He thought Sofia was by his side.

7

Come on, come and help me.

Three months earlier, at twelve-thirty one morning in February, *Frau* Mandel walked into the barrack 115 and, without ordering them to line up, bawled "You, you and you!" not haphazardly, but knowing who the weakest were, the ones to dispense with that day. Her words needed no explanation. They heard and started to shout and implore. They were beaten, pushed and shoved outside to join a row of women from other barracks. A total of 110 women, children and old people were led to the gas chamber.

The woman lying beside and embracing Sofia—Josefina Luftwig, the owner of the clothes shop in Krakow—has her eyes closed and mouth open, a dark, bottomless, repulsively human hole between lips as white as chalk. Sofia shares a similar rictus, that same private boundary that marks the end. They have just died and their bodies are in a pile with others in the gas chamber. The immeasurable closeness of bodies, Benjamin's words come to mind once again. Sofia and the woman embracing her are naked, their bones visible through their white skin. Remnants to be burnt quickly. Skeletal, angular extremities they sometimes must be broken to put them in the oven. Nothing remains, no wage for memory.

Then, finally, I wonder, rather obscenely, what might Sofia's last thought have been. I imagine her thinking of Ari, her son, that forlorn being who, when separated from his mother, came to be Hurbinek the Nameless, but perhaps she thought of Yakov, Yakov's love, smells and kisses. "Come on, come and help me," words connected to something he once said to her very tenderly, when he needed her, but where? Her time had run out. The rest was her heart beating fast, almost breaking out of her body. The horror.

XII

THE PLURAL LIFE OF OBJECTS

1
Clothes

The child they called Ari while Sofia, his mother, was alive, is Hurbinek again, the boy without a name. That child never left the camp, didn't escape, wasn't one of the children they smuggled out of Auschwitz with great difficulty, as Sofia preferred to believe before she died. He was picked up from under barrack 115, as planned by Gloria Monod, a skinny French Jewess who used to be a shop assistant in a big department store on the Champs Elysées, but she couldn't expedite the child's departure from the camp. If he'd died right then, frozen to death or skewered by one of the SS guards, nothing would have been altered in the chain of life: it was his natural fate in the day-to-day running of the camp. On the other hand, Gloria Monod also forged her own fate when she decided to keep him close. She used a high, hiding place in her barrack, a space hollowed out where the wood ceiling beams crossed, that only she had access to from the third tier of bunks, where she slept with five other women. However, that was a thin line between life and death. Gloria knew Hurbinek could fall or cry in her absence, and that's why she tied him to the beam with strips of cloth and put a gag in his mouth. When she returned to the barrack she never knew whether she would find the child dead or alive.

One of the first things Gloria Monod did with Hurbinek was to change his clothes. She got rid of the pieces of blanket that were wrapped round him when she found him, and dressed him in a kind of striped, woollen shirt, made from the prison uniform belonging to a young woman who'd died of diphtheria in her barrack. She also dressed him in a double jacket that was also striped, that was mended and re-sewn with bits of string and pieces of underwear torn into very thin strips. As they didn't have needles, the prisoners used wooden splinters they sharpened, or bit through the material and then sewed big darns with their fingers.

When I think of Hurbinek's short life, I cannot not avoid thinking about the objects he had or that accompanied him for that brief period. They were never entirely his: they came from someone else and would be passed on to someone else. In a way, he was an unconscious borrower of other people's objects. There could never be many. They would inevitably be few, very few, ordinary, common, basic materials at hand: rubber, leather, iron, wool and wood. I can imagine them now in a museum, on display in a glass cabinet, symbols and samples from many other people who used or possessed similar things. I imagine them in the museum in Auschwitz, or any other Holocaust museum, cold, distant but eloquent, offered to visitors as a slice of historical memory, visitors who struggle to locate them in the inconceivable reality to which they once belonged. I was going to Auschwitz, but not anymore. I won't see those objects, and yet, at night, here in my Frankfurt hospital bedroom, I see them clearly, I can see that cabinet, the light illuminating it, the line on the floor warning "don't cross" a few inches from the cabinet, the striped clothes on the body of a hollow dummy or doll made of transparent polyurethane. And I can't help thinking that, though the clothes are real, what's really important is the hollow inside of the invisible dummy wearing them, because that hollowness and dummy are the Jew or Gypsy, or even my Hurbinek.

But I know that only what has a name exists, and I want to name each detail, each insignificant detail of those objects, because they are what existed *with* Hurbinek, what gave his life substance. And when I see or imagine those clothes that once clad Hurbinek's tiny body or the objects that passed through his life, I imagine the possible histories of both clothes and objects. Where did they come from, who touched them, who owned them, who loved and used them before and after him? Who do those things belong to, in the end, in life? Can we speak of a *beloved* object when referring to clothes made from remnants of uniforms belonging to prisoners whose names are now impossible to trace, striped material that has never been washed, that carries vomit from Sarah, excrements from a fellow called Rufus or blood from some girl called Chana? Yes but, even so, those clothes Gloria Monod made for him were the only ones Hurbinek wore during the rest of his life.

2

A hat with ear flaps

The hat with earflaps that Gloria gave to Hurbinek, traded with a prisoner for her boots, had belonged to an eight-year-old boy—his name was Moniek Swajcer—the only survivor from his whole family in the selection made on the ramp where prisoners left the convoys, though he was beaten to death a month later.

It was a small, quite worn, leather, fur-lined hat. Its dark blue had faded and cracked. There were remnants of gold filigree on the foldable earflaps. Little Moniek had been given the hat for his fifth birthday by his father. The day when the boy was caught peeing outside the latrines by an eighteen-year-old SS who beat him to death with a mace encrusted at both ends with huge nails, the hat ended up in the hands of one of the women who distributed the food round the barracks and happened to be passing by. She didn't look up or at the dead boy. She was shaking as she retrieved the hat and put it away. She swapped it for Gloria's boots. Gloria was left barefoot, and had to manufacture boots from strips of felt and material collected at dawn from bodies that died every night; they weren't enough to resist the cold and the frosts. In the roll calls at twilight, that went on for hours out in the open, one of her feet froze. She lost all feeling in it, although the pain had been intolerable to that point. But she didn't complain; that way she would betray nothing. Even so, her frozen foot was the reason why she was selected for the gas chamber, when the female guard saw she was limping and that one of her feet was completely dead. They went out of their way to amputate before gassing her.

Hurbinek survived, cared for by the other prisoners, although it was risky. He was once mistaken for a bird, perhaps an owl or a smaller bird, when an SS looked up at the ceiling beams when she heard a noise. She thought she had heard wings flapping and aimed her gun at whatever was moving, but she could see nothing clearly from where she was standing. The prisoners didn't even look startled; they knew the child was condemned to die and would be found out at any moment: his time had come, period. Not one muscle tensed. But when the female guard was taking aim, convinced it was a bird, a pigeon or a jay maybe, she had second thoughts and lowered her gun, "I don't kill animals. When did that bird ever do me any harm? I go into the countryside when I want to hunt," she rasped as she left.

3

Soup bowl

A month later they disinfected the barrack because there were too many rats. They gnawed on the sick and the dead. They hauled out all the prisoners and kept them standing on the esplanade for forty-eight hours. They could only sit down for one hour in every twelve. They were forced to stand for the rest of that time. Several elderly women died of exhaustion. Others were shot in the neck because they squatted or kneeled down. The women looking after Hurbinek, Gloria's companions in the third level of bunk beds, aware of the secret, hidden child, assumed that boy would be poisoned when he breathed in the disinfectant dust. Besides, there were three other children hidden like him. But when they returned to the barrack two days later, they found that Hurbinek— what name did they call him by? None perhaps, names create bonds, create affection—was still alive, very undernourished and dirty, and almost at death's door. The other three children had died. They didn't have a mother; the women who were crying and had hidden them weren't their mothers. Perhaps, like Hurbinek, they were children who'd had to stay there after they failed to smuggle them out of the camp. One woman started to give him little sips of watery potato soup, using a chipped enameled metal bowl, the edge of which was painted red, that was rusty in parts, including the handle. They had no spoons, or only one to share among several prisoners.

That bowl that brushed little Hurbinek's lips for many weeks had been manufactured in the center of Cologne, by Julius Hölderbruner Industries, Karlstrasse, 17, that specialized in equipment for the Wehrmacht and came from a consignment of items "for domestic use," as it said in the order requesting 150,000 bowls signed first by R. Höss, the camp commandant, and underneath, in second place, by A. Eichmann. Before it belonged to the woman who fed Hurbinek, it had been owned in the concentration camp by Anita Sachs (who engraved her name on the bottom of the bowl) and Gloria Monod. After the death of its last anonymous owner, the bowl rusted completely and was buried, with other useless bits of crockery, in a ditch near the barbed wire fence. A Russian soldier, Ivan Rutilov, stumbled over it in March, 1945 when he was walking around the Auschwitz camp looking for a target for a spot of shooting practice. He dug it up and threw it into the air. A salvo of bullets from his pistol filled it with five holes.

Soon after the barrack had been disinfected, at the end of 1943, the prisoners decided to put an end to Hurbinek's suffering, and they agreed that one of them would deposit him in the latrines, next to a pile of bricks the top of which had a spout that stuck out and served as a kind of shower. If one of the female guards found him, he was sure to die, but perhaps another woman prisoner would take him in. What would she do with that child? Perhaps hand him over? What was the point of living like that? In any case, they trusted in her pity, although the price of mercy in Auschwitz was high. On the other hand, chance came cheap. It would be down to luck. So they left Hurbinek to his.

4

Shoes

It was a long time before Hurbinek had any shoes. In the middle of January 1944 young Ruchel Szlezinger made him some by adapting those that had once belonged to Miriam, her eight-year-old sister, who was taken aside upon arriving in the camp and eliminated.

She managed to keep hold of them because she had a little bundle of the two sisters' belongings she hid under her clothes. Miriam's shoes were black, made from good leather, with round toecaps and laces that tied by the bottom of the ankle. Little Miriam Szlezinger had cleaned them the night before she was arrested and they still retained some of that shine. Ruchel adopted the shoes to Hurbinek's tiny feet by packing the toes with material she folded over several times, and then plaited the laces around the baby's legs so the shoes didn't rub and make them sore.

Ruchel and Miriam Szlezinger were the daughters of a Prague doctor who was sent with his wife to the camp in Theresienstadt. The two sisters ended up in Auschwitz because of a transportation error; it didn't matter much, they were all going to die anyway. Dr. Szlezinger was well off and paid the Gestapo in order to preserve his freedom after the assassination of Heydrich in 1941, but when his capital—the the proceeds from jewels that had been inherited across many generations—dried up, he and his family were brutally deported.

They bought Miriam's shoes in 1940. They'd been on display in a shopwindow in Mala Strana for several days; nobody took any interest in them until little Miriam, out for a walk with her parents, fell in love with them. They had to pay for them in marks from the Reich, though the Szlezingers couldn't do so directly, because Jews couldn't buy anything, and so a Czech woman, the nurse who helped Szlezinger, did it for them. They'd been manufactured in Munich in a factory expropiated from a Jewish family murdered in Bergen-Belsen. Thus, the only real shoes Hurbinek wore in his short life were German shoes, probably made by a happy woman, convinced she was an honest soul, whose husband perhaps belonged to a Police Batallion heading to the Ukraine or Lithuania and responsible for carrying out racial cleansing.

Young Ruchel picked up Hurbinek out of compassion, moved by the loving memory of her sister, the day after an anonymous hand had deposited him in the latrines by the water spout. It was a misty, very cold, winter's day. She had to warm him with her breath, rubbing his arms and legs, and immediately began to scheme so they wouldn't catch her with him. She knew that children's lives were of no value in that place, because they couldn't work; she knew that was why they had *sacrificed* Miriam, since Rachel felt all that death surrounding her was a sacrifice Yaveh demanded of his people, an absurd sacrifice like all the other words that issued from the mouths of rabbis. The lives of children were soon snuffed out in a mere clout, a squeeze of the neck, or by hurling them against a post.

Taking all kinds of precautions, though guided by a gloomy, unfathomable presentiment, she finally hid him cleverly inside her straw mattress. He stayed there until June, 1944, when they searched Ruchel's barrack for a rudimentary radio apparatus via which the women prisoners had heard that the Americans had disembarked in France. The SS didn't find the radio in the barrack; however, they did find Hurbinek, two years, three months and three days after he was born.

5

Blanket

They were human whimpers and this time the guard didn't mistake them for a cat or bird. They were inarticulate whimpers, not even crying, more like a striving effort, a soft click, a kind of shout or barely audible affirmation of life. It was coming from the meagre mattress of one of the prisoners, a young woman with a scarf around her head and a look of terror in her eyes that she intuited would be her last. It was Ruchel. When they extracted him from the mattress, from the straw, he was tightly wrapped in a blanket. Ruchel had thought of re-shaping that thick material to cover him better, perhaps giving it sleeves, a collar, or shaping it, she hadn't gone to dress-making classes in Prague for nothing, but she never had the time or energy in those months.

It was a gray blanket bordered by a labyrinth of yellow geometric shapes. It wasn't a blanket given out by the *Waffen SS*, but a blanket brought at the last moment by a prisoner. It belonged to a Greek family, the Karaindrous, from Salonika. The head of the family had grabbed it instinctively when they were forced to leave their houses at gunpoint, and had thrown it over the shoulder of his middle son, who, in turn, in the cattle truck, gave it to an old woman who was shivering in one corner. That meant the woman didn't freeze to death that day. In the camp, when the old woman's heart stopped beating while she was asleep, Ruchel took it before the others snatched the rest of her clothes.

It was a good quality blanket that ended up in tatters in a Soviet camp, where the female SS guard died five years later, the one who took Hurbinek by the arm after stripping him of his blanket and lifted him up like a young pup to bang him against the little brick wall that ran acrosss the barrack.

And she would have done so—it wouldn't have been the first time—if it hadn't been for a lean, wily Jewish helper in the *Lagerarzt,* who was forced to be present at all the roll calls and participate in the cruel search for booty, deformed men and women, twins, hidden children, or people with some physical peculiarity. She thought that child with its tiny, still body that looked atrophied, with his sunken eyes, was the most wretched, defeated being in the world, and would be a suitable item. A sinister smile spread over her face, though it wasn't at all proud. That trophy would improve her position; it would give her a partial reprieve, they wouldn't kill her, yet.

As for Ruchel Szlezinger, the girl with the shining, intelligent eyes, she was sent to the gas chamber within an hour. They applied the usual, horrific practice, the routine immolation of her innocence, that now no longer stirred the remaining survivors in the emotional wasteland that was Auschwitz. Hurbinek, for his part, would lose his shoes in Dr. Mengele's infirmary; it wouldn't matter because by then his legs would have lost all feeling.

6

A wooden doll

There was a toy in section B2a of the barrack given over to Mengele's experiments, a rough-and-ready toy, handmade by a puppet maker like Geppetto de Collodi. It was a wooden doll that had lost most of its original colors: the slender body of a fairy-tale prince. A gypsy girl had taken it there. Mengele had given the girl's skin radiation treatment to the point of producing burns that gradually spread over the rest of her skin, from the calves to the base of her neck. The girl died after two weeks. The wooden doll began to be used by Mengele and his collaborators as a means to calm the disconsolate sobbing of the children they were experimenting on. It was perhaps the only toy in Auschwitz and acted as a bait.

Children of different ages were housed in an outbuilding with bars like a big laboratory cage for mice. Several small white beds made that prison seem aseptic and scientific, but they were insufficient to take all the prisoners they lodged there, sometimes for months, depending on the nature of the experiment. Hurbinek stayed with Mengele for four months. He was tortured in various ways: they first focused on his food and weight, that was incredibly low, with progressive increases and reductions in the amount they gave him; then Mengele spent ages studying his anatomy before injecting him with controlled dosages of petrol, but then decided not to, although he did consider—made a note in his notebook to that end—boiling him and then extracting his bones and reconstructing him. However, he was finally chosen for a bone graft onto his spine. The operation was carried out without any medical precautions or concerns for his health, something that never worried Mengele. He kept him under observation for four or five weeks after the operation. It was a miracle he survived such torture.

Hurbinek had the wooden doll in his possession for a few days after he was brought to Mengele's barrack, but it was then taken away from him. He got it back after the operation. During those weeks the boy gripped the doll tight and tried to wail when it fell on the ground, though he never succeeded. A nurse would give it back to him and Hurbinek would stare endlessly at the doll, scrutinising the cracks in its red cape and the blue circles on the trousers or gold brushstrokes on the crown. What could any of that mean to him? I can't begin to imagine how curiosity develops in the midst of such torment.

One day toward the end of autumn, Mengele leaned over Hurbinek and took the doll from him and threw it far away. The small doll broke into two. Then two women grabbed Hurbinek and put him on a battered stretcher in the passageway, near the back door. Mengele had decided to let him die once septicemia from his spinal injuries set in. Mengele forbade any kind of cure. When the baby disappeared from his stretcher, nobody missed him; they assumed someone had taken him to the crematorium.

7

Buttons

Ángela Pérez León was a Spanish Sephardic Jew who'd been living in Bohemia since the end of the civil war. She suffered as she wondered what could be the purpose behind that senseless phase of history that had come her way. She couldn't forgive, wasn't able to garner more hatred, but was in such a state of defeat that many mornings, when the cold of dawn met the blue light of the new day, she anxiously strived to believe she must already be dead. The next moment of reality for her was the worst, most cruel torture that could be inflicted on the remnants of humanity everyone in the camp had become.

In Auschwitz Ángela had the misfortune to belong to the group of women prisoners forced to do support work in a *Sonderkommando*. She stripped the corpses in section B2a, Mengele's infirmary, before other Jews piled them up on a barrow and burned them in the open air, in a wood behind Crematorium V in Birkenau, when the ovens couldn't keep pace that winter. She was the person who took Hurbinek, still alive, to her barrack, 346, where she looked after and protected him until Christmas Eve, 1944, when *SS Obergruppenführer* Heinz Rügen walked in, found the child and shot her in the back of the neck. She was also the woman who introduced buttons into Hurbinek's life.

Ángela removed the jacket from the corpse of a five-year-old boy, Mosze Gold, one of Mengele's victims alongside Gavrilo, his twin brother. The woolen jacket had mother-of-pearl buttons, five large iridescent buttons the size of a small coin. Hurbinek touched them, in all likelihood, and felt their warm, polished surface, since that jacket stayed with him until he died. Marx was right when he said that social relations exist between objects, because those buttons had been manufactured in Denmark from seashells brought from Jamaica—that place Yakov Pawlicka so longed for—and had been imported by a Polish firm in 1938. The mother of the Gold twins bought the buttons in a haberdashery in Krakow next door to the Merkur Hotel on Krakowska Street where Yakov and Sofia checked in for their honeymoon, and sewed them on the jacket she herself had made for Mosze. She chose silvery buttons for Gavrilo. How could that mother ever have imagined that those Jamaican mother-of-pearl buttons would end up between the small, clumsy fingers of a dying child whose only homeland was that sewer of horror and rottenness? After Hurbinek died, Henek, who picked him up from the snow where Heinz Rügen had thrown him, kept this knitted jacket for many years, until he finally forgot it on his nth move, as one leaves behind things that no longer belong to anyone. However, he did pull off a button which he always kept on a silver chain round his neck.

8

Scarf

The last object in Hurbinek's imaginary museum is a scarf a Russian soldier tied round his sweaty, feverish forehead, when the camp was liberated. The scarf, as I picture it now in my imagination, or as it really must appear among Lucia Levi's possessions, is clean and ironed: it isn't very big, there are frayed threads at the corners and small tears; its ivory color has almost, but not quite, faded, and you can still make out the drawing of a Chinese dragon in the center. Hurbinek first wore it round his head like a ribbon—Henek would put it on and remove it—and later, days before he died, he put it around his neck to warm him up because he was shivering so much.

It was the young soldier Yuri Chanicheverov who put it on Hurbinek one day in early March 1945, after he entered the infirmary-barrack and found the dying child between Henek and Levi, who were caressing him. Disturbed and moved by the scene, he first soaked it in water from his water-flask. He thought something cool would do him good.

Yuri's sister Zhenia had given him the scarf she had bought in Moscow the day he left for the front as a souvenir. Yuri always wore it like a bracelet on the sleeve of his combat jacket. After Hurbinek died, when Henek and Yetzev went to bury him under that big tree, Levi removed the scarf from his neck and hid it inside the sleeve of his striped uniform. It carried an ambiguous smell of ammonia and persistent damp.

Primo Levi began writing about Hurbinek from that moment. He knew nothing about the child's past and refused to hazard any impossible future for him. However, the dirty scarf and its dragon stuck in his memory forever.

Levi survived his suffering and a year later, back in Turin, washed and ironed the scarf himself, and put it with other objects thrown up by life in a small, locked wooden box he would only open very occasionally. "Look at it, look how it enshrines everything and enshrines nothing," he would often be on the point of saying. But Lucia Levi, his widow, never really did work out what that old scarf was doing there among the things her husband kept so tidily. Finally, she spread it over a small stand beneath a flowerpot of red and yellow verbenas.

XIII

THE TREE OF PHOTOS FROM THIS WORLD

1

The night nurse on the sixth floor in Frankfurt's Universitäts-Kliniken woke me up this morning. I could swear he was singing and that I heard his crooning. The street lamps on Theodor Sternstrasse are still glowering, a dim, suspicious yellow I associate with discomfort, low voltage and disappearances. I'm numb and the plaster casts are excruciating. It's my last day here. Voghs, the ambivalent Dr. Voghs, will come at noon and summarily discharge me, after all these weeks, with no more moratoria, checks or analyses, as if I had been exposed as an impostor. I bet that in his childhood my doctor was one of the children who appear in photos of the time surrounding Hitler, saluting and waving their little red swastika flags. Then he'll ask, averting his gaze, whether I'm thinking of continuing on my tourist route and will recommend a drive to Heidelberg, for example. "It's my city. I'm sure you will really like its streets. They are very picturesque. They weren't bombed." I will reply by asking if he really thinks that in my state, with two crutches and a chest hurting from a broken rib, I'm up to wandering around touristy streets. He'll say, still averting his gaze, that the jury is still out on that one.

When the night nurse made me open my eyes because of his humming and noise, I was dreaming. I wasn't dreaming a dream of my own, but Hurbinek's, that is if he ever managed to dream. You can be sure he only had nightmares in his subconscious, at most an animal, liquid dream of being in Sofia's lap, his brief, unique feeling of pleasure in life. I know what that's like. I once woke Zoe my daughter up when she was in the middle of a nightmare and now remember her hugs and trembling, her mysterious gratitude, fearful smile and gradual shift to a happier, wakeful reality. Hurbinek felt none of this. Perhaps Henek cradled and comforted him out of his bad dreams, toward the end of his life; that was probably good Henek's nighttime, conscientious undertaking, but it was already too late.

Primo Levi says people in Auschwitz dreamed of hunger. It was the continuation of the same thought they had when awake. The fortress of our dreams, the place where no one else can enter, quickly collapsed when exhaustion sunk prisoners into the precious trance of sleep. Their tiny capital soon ran out, because hunger immediately surfaced and woke them up, or followed a strategy of keeping them asleep as if that were yet another torture that forced them to experience unconsciously the same unpleasant reality they faced when awake. As if decided by some painfully cruel decree, dreams in Auschwitz were circular, couldn't be distinguished from wakefulness, you dreamed and you woke up, you woke up and you dreamed, not knowing where one state began and another ended. They didn't divide time into day and night, but immersed it in permanent, ambiguous confusion: reality as nightmare, nightmare as reality.

The dream the nurse woke me from was a dream I'd borrowed, like Walter Benjamin's when he thought he was someone else, an anguished mathematician dreaming that a legion of ants ate a lizard in a minute and then calculated how many lizards can be consumed in a month, a year, a whole life-time, and how long it would take to consume that whole world species of lizard and how many ants it would take to wipe the lizards off the face of the earth. In *my* dream—that was really Hurbinek's—I remembered every single person I had known in my life, everyone I had ever come across, if only once. A glance, or a touch was enough. Each face I'd seen, each voice I'd heard, every detail of clothing, every gesture I'd registered. Every individual, good, bad and indifferent. My dream was exhaustive; a face appeared and immediately revived the moment our lives had crossed. Everything I had forgotten gradually erupted in my dream. It was like a task I had to complete, I knew I was working on that assignment and still had many people to remember. It was an exhausting dream. And a photo of each and every one of these people was hanging from a tree. Hurbinek and myself were standing under a large, leafy tree, and he was saying they were going to bury him under that tree. I looked up and saw thousands of photos sticking out from between its branches. I then remembered "Hurbinek's tree" as Henek called the story that he later invented for his son Stanislazh.

2

I am getting my things ready. The consul assured me he would drive me to the airport. I will ask him to drive me around the city beforehand. I want to pass by the Alte Oper in a vain hunt for Heinz Rügen's house. It is simply my inevitable curiosity, something akin to walking on the brink of a precipice and looking over. I don't know which house will be his or what it will look like. It's probably that hotel I am imagining, perhaps one by the name of Helvetia—neutral names, to avoid stupid allegiances, the German post-war stance, etc.—and Rügen's widow, a seventy-year-old blonde who goes for a swim every afternoon in the public swimming pool, is now married to a fine upstanding man who returned depressed from the front, a fine orderly policeman who benefited from state grants and US aid, and various pardons, the usual looking the other way Germans so appreciate. First he opened a tavern and then a boarding house, and later when the city became so prosperous, what with its fairs and its banks, the boarding house became a hotel, initially quite small, but then he extended it, had to take on more staff, although none would be his new wife's children, the children of *SS Obergruppenführer* Rügen. Both now enjoy a pension and are good citizens of Europe with democratic views in matters of environmental policy.

I have seen photos of certain Auschwitz camp guards, members of the *Waffen SS*, photos that must surely hang from the tree of photos in Hurbinek's dream. They are very young, almost innocent out of sheer youth, at most eighteen or twenty years old. Nonetheless, they have that cold, cruel, perfectly superior look. The SS insignia on the jacket collars of their uniforms eloquently denotes pride and obedience. They can kill and hold their heads up high. They can kill everybody. Nothing and nobody will stop them. I can imagine each committing some kind, any kind of atrocity. And yet not one has been executed, tried or arrested. So if they haven't died from an old people's ailment in their beds, surrounded by their family, after a life lived to the fullest, I may meet them now when I walk out into the street, still quite chipper fifty or sixty years on, retired from work, schoolmasters, professors, engineers, mechanics, traders, civil servants working for the Federal Republic or Lander, car salesmen, taxi drivers or bank employees. They are all out there in the street. They all had long lives, enjoyed many birthdays and are full of little stories they love to tell.

I still don't know why a character from the hospital came to take my photo when I was still wearing the green nightshirt, and standing with the help of my crutches. The nurse tells me it's do with insurance, because the Universitäts-Kliniken cannot cover the cost of my stay. I feel stupid on these crutches, almost naked, barely covered by my patient's garb. Unwantingly, I feel as if I am a victim, that I've suffered far too much, though the truth is the only thing that's happened is that I've been in hospital for a short period of time, and have not exactly been badly treated. It's all been quite straightforward, considering that I could now be dead on that wretched stretch of motorway. I wonder what strange metamorphosis I've undergone. Was it my truncated trip to Auschwitz, being held powerless and paralyzed in Frankfurt, or perhaps the rarefied atmosphere in this hospital, all mixed up with my thoughts as I invented Hurbinek's lives? The Russians entered Auschwitz in January, 1945 and took thousands of photos. Photos of the remains, of corpses, of the emaciated bodies of the survivors. Photos of those driven mad. Photos of those who'd been hung. Photos of the wretched. Photos of ill-covered mass graves. A vast album of an immense funeral. Photos containing nothing honorable: destructive, accusing, inhuman photos. Photos of debris. Photos showing irrefutable examples, to be wielded against any possible lies. Photos that at number one thousand become monotonous. Photos so there is no need to use your imagination. Photos of this world. Photos, to a point, "for the insurance," like mine in that hospital. The time for penitence, then, began with those photos.

After getting dressed I went over and said goodbye to my roommate, Oskar, who listens to music all the time, speaks English and constantly reads sports papers. He will be left by himself. There were three empty beds and now, with mine, there will be four. They'll soon fill them I expect. His hip is shattered, and a truck was to blame, as it was in my case. It happened in a tunnel on Autobahn A-3, the same one where I had my accident. That detail means we have something in common. When I shake his hand, I hear music that I recognize on his headphones.

"Jazz. Always Helen Merrill," he says with a smile. "My father played with her. From Chicago. My father, I mean. I'm not, my mother and I are Germans, from here. I was listening to that in the tunnel, at the time of the crash. I didn't register a thing."

"I was listening to Leonard Cohen," I say.

"He was a Jew, wasn't he?"

"Apparently."

Music and coincidences. March 3, 1945, Dimitri Yeliptkin, a soldier in the Third Division of the Red Army, who never knew of Hurbinek's existence, set up an old gramola in the Main Camp in Auschwitz, put a record on, turned the handle and took a photo while it played Mozart's *Requiem*. "I wanted to photograph the music," he said. As coincidence would have it, he did so the day that Hurbinek died.

I left the room very slowly, and then left the hospital equally slowly.

3

I have often wondered why Primo Levi didn't take Hurbinek further, why he thought two pages were enough to bear witness to his life, why he decided not to investigate his life, and years later find out where that child came from, the truth, in other words, that Hurbinek was in fact Ari Pawlicka. However, today I think Primo Levi did, he did take it further, as far as he could.

Perhaps it happened like this.

Perhaps on a day late in October, 1955 Primo Levi happened to leave home in the middle of the morning, as usual, and went to the Post Office where he had a post box. He found a letter from Henek, who was living in Budapest at the time under his real name, Belo König. In this letter, Henek answered the question Primo Levi had asked in a previous one about how far it might be possible to find real data on Hurbinek's family, since he thought it was only right to give that short, tortured life a history, and it was making his dreams unbearably painful. Henek wrote that from what he had later been able to find out, there had been 114 cases like Hurbinek's in Auschwitz, and that he too was obsessed by the void in the past of that baby boy they'd cared for and buried. He decided to find out more, now that times had drifted into a kind of amnesia, and told Levi he had initiated a rough-and-ready search for information, asking around in circles of ex-prisoners, with the help of Polish friends. Soon, he said he would at least be able to tell him what city he came from, which ghetto, and then it would be easier to get closer to the district and family. Primo Levi and Henek sustained correspondence over a couple of months. Levi tried to dissuade him from jumping to the conclusion that it would be easy to find this out, although in fact Henek never managed to give him any specific name, or any of the more specific details he optimistically promised in each letter. He was on the brink, he would say, and that was all. He seemed to be going in and out of the same maze. Then a long time went by, several months of complete silence, and Henek's letters stopped coming. Then, one midday when a blizzard of snow was blowing Primo Levi opened his post box and found a letter from Budapest, but from Henek's wife, Claricia, not from Henek. She wrote very sparingly that Henek had died. So as far as Levi was concerned, his friend's investigations into the origins of Hurbinek remained inconclusive, although he sometimes imagined when re-reading his letters, that the courageous Henek had never had any more than good intentions, or perhaps a mutual attempt to salvage the memory of little Hurbinek, erased forever from the map of Europe, like that of his entire people.

Yes, perhaps that is what happened.

4

I'm coming to the end and am still the naïve birthday buyer for Hurbinek. I shall soon depart from this country where "death is a German Master," as in Paul Celan's famous line. A few more words and I will be gone.

In the tree of photos from Hurbinek's dreams there are two photos on which my gaze lingers as I wait for the Spanish consul leaning on my crutches under the canopy over the hospital entrance, motionless and invisible like a ghost in the eyes of passers-by.

One of the photos is of Sofia standing in a park in Rzeszów, next to the castle. It was taken by an itinerant photographer. Sofia is eighteen years old; she is wearing a small, plain hat on the tilt, almost like a helmet. It was a present from her aunt Mikaela. Her head is slightly bowed, she is smiling shyly and lifting her right hand to say hello. She is carrying a handbag on her forearm that's made of small pieces of metal like a kind of chain mail. Her gloved left hand is clasping her other glove. It is a nondescript photo, like many others that could have been taken that afternoon in that park, like so many others Sofia no doubt possessed. It is a happy photo she always carried with her and left in the Krakow ghetto when they were forced to leave the house in a rush. It was lost among the debris from the building when the Nazis demolished it soon after, and was then retrieved by someone who found it among the garbage in a rubble site and kept on a whim, someone or other who never knew her, who looks at it and wonders who that woman might be. It is a photo Hurbinek would never see.

The other photo is my accident. I am lying on the hard shoulder of Autobahn A-3. A bright metal sheet apparently made of silver is covering my head and torso. You can see my shoes and part of my trousers. A few feet away, you can catch a glimpse of part of my car, smashed up, its wheels up in the air. The feet of other people, perhaps nurses or police, intrude in one corner. "There is no hope," might be a caption for the photo. It could be anybody's corpse, but I have no doubt that it is mine. It is a photo of me where you can see that I am dead. Or so they said. Perhaps I was born anew that day, perhaps Hurbinek was born anew with me as well. That's why the photo is hanging there on the tree in that strange dream.

I see the consul driving up at last, and say to myself, "Goodbye Frankfurt, goodbye hospital, goodbye century." I make my escape via the car door. I'm going home. Really?

Primo Levi returned to Turin on October 19 in the same year that Hurbinek died. He writes that his house was just as he left it and that no one was expecting him. No one in his family recognized him at first when they saw him he was so changed. He took a long time to rid himself of the anguish in his dreams. I haven't changed over these weeks, and my daughters will easily recognize me, I am sure, but deep down I *have* really changed. Perhaps it is a subtle change, as they say of men who suddenly grow old or mature. I have re-visited the last century, I have entered into its horrors and imagined its gray epicenter in the short life of little Hurbinek, the three-year-old Jewish boy. Thinking, researching and telling all that has changed me. Of course it has.

I now know for sure: I was going to Auschwitz, but not anymore.

DEDICATION

This novel is dedicated to the memory of Scholomo Buczko, Belo König, Rubem Yetzev, Abrahan Levine, Elias Achtzehn, Ernst Sterman, Chaim Roth, Ira Roth, Prosper Andlauer, Franz Patzold, Jan Vesely, Ahmed Yildirim, Manuel Valiño, David Bogdanowski, Joseph Grosselin, Auguste Friedel, Konrad Egger, Berek Goldstein, Sofia Cèrmik, Yakov Pawlicka, Ari Pawlicka, Aaron Cèrmik, Stefan Cèrmik, Samuel Pawlicka, David Pawlicka, Gork Vigo, Sara Zelman, Mikaela Zelman, Gus Lazar, Ansel Block, Artur Sugar, Frankie Sugar, Simon Azvel, Josefina Luftig, Sara Ruda Malach, Barbara Breonka, Ada Neufeld, Gloria Monod, Moniek Swajcer, Anita Sachs, Ángela Pérez León, Ruchel Szlezinger, Miriam Szlezinger, Mosze Gold and Gavrilo Gold, who lived under other names.

TRANSLATOR'S NOTE

The translation of Paul Celan is from *Paul Celan. Poet, Survivor, Jew* by John Felstiner, Yale University Press, 2001.

The translations from *If This Is a Man* and *The Truce* by Primo Levi are from the translations by Stuart Woolf, Penguin Books, 1979.

ABOUT THE AUTHOR

ADOLFO GARCÍA ORTEGA has been involved in the world of books and literature since 1980, as a translator, editor, literary critic and journalist. He regularly contributes to the Spanish newspaper *El País* and is currently Associate Publishing Director of the Planeta Publishing Group. He has a distinguished reputation as a writer, and his diverse output includes poetry, fiction and nonfiction works. The novels *Lobo*, *Desolation Island*, *Café Hugo*, *The Birthday Buyer* and *Pasajero K*, have all brought him considerable public and critical acclaim, receiving major awards as well as being widely translated. His latest fiction work is the collection of stories *Verdaderas historias extraordinarias*.

ABOUT THE TRANSLATOR

PETER BUSH is an award-winning translator who lives in Barcelona. His translations from Spanish include Valle-Inclán's *Tyrant Banderas*, García Lorca's *Sketches of Spain: Impressions and Landscapes*, and García Ortega's *Desolation Island*. His translation of Quim Monzó's *A Thousand Morons* is just out and other fiction from Catalan will soon follow: his wife Teresa Solana's *The Sound of One Hand Killing* and Mercè Rodoreda's *In Diamond Square*. His first translation was Juan Goytisolo's *Forbidden Territory*. He has translated a dozen books by Goytisolo and is currently working on his poetry.

Made in the USA
Lexington, KY
02 June 2015